SWEAT, BLOOD, SUCCESS

CHRISTOPHER STEPHEN VERMA

English (Indian)

Title: SWEAT, BLOOD, SUCCESS

Author: CHRISTOPHER STEPHEN VERMA

ISBN: 9798303894921

Published on: 23/12/2024

The views and contents of this book are solely of the author. This book is being sold on the condition and understanding that its contents are merely for information and reference and that neither the author nor the publishers, printers or sellers of this book are engaged in rendering legal, accounting, or other professional service. The author, publisher and printer specifically disclaim all any liability for any loss, damage, risk, injury, distress, etc. suffered by an person, whether or not a purchaser of this book, as a consequence whether direct or indirect, of any action taken or not taken on the basis of the contents of this book. This publisher believes that the contents of this book do not violate any existing copyright/ intellectual property of others in any manner whatsoever. However, in the event the author has been unable to track any source and if any copyright has been inadvertently infringed, please notify the publisher in writing for corrective action.

Published by:

In Association with

DIGITAL WRITOPRENEURS HUB AND ACADEMY, NEW DELHI

Mob: 91 72918 49502

About the Author

Born into a middle-class Defence family, Christopher Verma's life was far from a bed of roses. After a challenging yet successful education, owed primarily to the frequent transfer of his father's work. Both in India and overseas, at a young tender age of 18, Chris found out the bitter realities of life. With ambitions of becoming a doctor being dashed, he struggled on the streets of Mumbai, through all the challenges of commuting, getting work, corrupt system, cheats, and above all an empty pocket, his journey left him with deep scars. With one square meal a day, he fought his way, keeping just one point in mind - I AM NOT A QUITTER; failure is a part of life, a part of learning. The more you fall the stronger you get. Until one day, the Universe heard him. There was no looking back there on till the end. In spite and despite the pitfalls, he kept getting up and turned his life around. One success led to another.

He thus embarked on a new journey, to educate, teach, and motivate people on how to break away from the shackles of the "social norms" and live your own dreams. To understand that there is NO IMPOSSIBLE, if only we choose to see it as I'M POSSIBLE. Life is about Acceptance and not Expectance; it's not about what we don't have, but to cherish what we do have. To know, understand and master the biggest, most sophisticated machine on this planet...OUR BODY.

His mission over the past 15 years has and continues to be " GIVING BACK TO THE WORLD".

After the tremendous success of creating your ultimate bliss and the book 'Transcending the Transaction World', became a Number 1 bestseller, this book, ‘Sweat, Blood, Success’ is his next work.

Dedication

This book is dedicated...

To my lifelong friends, who have
laughed with me, cried with me,
and made memories that will last a
lifetime. I'm so grateful to have you
all in my life.
This book is specifically dedicated to my closest friends,
who have been my
partners in crime, my confidantes
and my biggest cheerleaders. You have seen me at my
best and worst, and still choose to be my friend; and
who know the chapters I left unsaid.
Here's to many more years of
love, laughter, and making more
unforgettable memories together.

Synopsis

There goes an old saying that 'Tough times make tough people'. What's not said is that 'Tumultuous times make for terrific stories!'

Some people are born to endure struggles, even including life threating moments in the bargain. This is one such story where the protagonist Chetan has more than his fair share of undeserved misery and yet triumphs it with steely resolve to achieve tremendous success and admiration. It's also a story of his childhood friendship with Aryan, who faces equal amounts of turmoil in his life, if not more, and how their friendship becomes an integral part of their lives, helping them overcome even the toughest of times.

Contents

CHAPTER 1
THE REUNION

I arrived at my workplace, a vast warehouse facility located on the outskirts of a bustling shipping town, precisely at nine o'clock in the morning, just as I always did. The rhythmic routine of my mornings grounded me, and today was no different. As I walked through the entrance, I exchanged a friendly smile with the receptionist at the front desk, acknowledging her cheerful greeting. It was a small gesture, but one that set a positive tone for the day ahead.

After a brief moment of small talk, I stepped into the elevator, the doors sliding shut with a quiet whoosh. The sleek machine whisked me up to the fourth floor, where my office awaited me. Once I arrived, I pushed open the door to my cabin, stepping inside with a sense of purpose.

I settled into my well-worn office chair, the familiar leather embracing me as I faced my expansive desk. My workspace was meticulously organized, reflecting my methodical nature. My laptop sat at the centre, a vital tool for managing the intricate operations of the company. To the side, a printer hummed softly, ready to produce the documents I needed for meetings and presentations. A multi-line office phone, its buttons worn from frequent use, stood at the ready, an essential lifeline for communicating with partners, clients, and colleagues around the globe.

Stationery supplies—pens, notepads, and paperweights—were neatly arranged, ensuring that everything I needed was within arm's reach. Beside me, an empty coffee mug rested on a side table, a silent reminder of my early morning ritual. It had been filled with my favourite brew; a strong dark roast that helped fuel my busy day.

Behind me, an impressive bookshelf stretched from floor to ceiling, a testament to my dedication to continuous learning. The shelves were packed with hundreds of books on various topics, from Business Management to Politics, Industrial Law, and Health and Nutrition. Each title represented hours of study and contemplation, contributing to the depth of knowledge I wielded in my role.

The office reflected my status perfectly. As the CEO of one of the world's largest merchant shipping companies, I understood the importance of projecting authority and professionalism. Every detail in the room—from the elegant decor to the organized chaos of paperwork—was curated to inspire confidence in those who entered. It was more than just an office; it embodied my commitment to excellence and leadership in the ever-evolving maritime industry. Today, like every day, I was ready to tackle the challenges that lay ahead, steering my company toward new horizons.

I was a man of stringent discipline, a quality that shaped both my personal and professional life. I thrived on immersing myself in work, driven by an unwavering determination to achieve whatever goals I set my sights on. This relentless pursuit stemmed from the struggles I had faced in my early life, where each challenge had only strengthened my resolve. Those experiences instilled in me a fierce work ethic and a commitment to never give up, no matter how daunting the task at hand.

My passion for fitness was another cornerstone of my disciplined lifestyle. Every morning, I would rise before dawn, lacing up my running shoes for a jog through the quiet streets. The rhythmic pounding of my feet against the pavement was both a physical and mental warm-up for the day ahead. When time allowed, I'd make my way to the gym, pushing my limits with each workout. Maintaining my health and fitness was non-negotiable; it was an essential part of who I was.

Even in the office, my discipline was evident. I sat with impeccable posture, my back straight and shoulders squared, a posture I maintained regardless of the demands of the day. I hated to recline, feeling that a relaxed posture might undermine the seriousness with which I approached my responsibilities. In fact, I had taken the extra step of locking my expensive office chair to prevent it from reclining fully. However, the chair did offer a slight give, and today was one of those rare occasions when I found myself leaning back, my hands folded behind my head in a moment of rare respite.

But even as I rested against the chair, my mind was anything but at ease. I mulled over the complexities of a particularly troubling situation that had recently arisen in the company.

There were pressing problems that required immediate attention, and I knew I couldn't afford to delay any longer. My warehouse and factory were under complete lockdown, a situation that was becoming increasingly dire. For the past ten days, the labourers had been on strike, a protest that not only stalled production but also paralyzed the entire operation. Transport consignments, crucial for my business, were stranded and barricaded, leaving me with no clear path forward.

To make matters worse, I had been receiving a barrage of death threats, a grim reality that weighed heavily on my mind. It all started with an anonymous phone call late one night. I had just settled into bed after a long day, the soft hum of family laughter still echoing in my mind, when the shrill ring of the landline shattered the tranquillity.

"Chetan," a low voice rasped, sending a chill down my spine. "You and your goddamn company have no reason for being on our lands. You both aren't going to survive much longer. Watch your back." The line went dead before I could even respond. My heart raced, and I turned to Jean, who was already awake, concern etched across her face.

"Who was it?" she asked, her voice trembling.

"I don't know," I replied, my mind racing. "But it sounded serious."

The following days were filled with tension. I tried to brush off the call, attributing it to a prank or a disgruntled associate. I focused on my work, pouring myself into projects at the shipping company, trying to ignore the nagging feeling in the back of my mind. But then the letters started arriving.

They were slipped under the door of my office, the envelopes unmarked. The first one was vague, just a warning: "You're in over your head. Get out while you still can." My instincts kicked in; this was no coincidence.

The second letter was more direct. "We know where you live. We know your family. We don't think your family and you will be safe for much longer." A sense of dread washed over me, tightening its grip around my heart. I couldn't shake the feeling that someone was watching, lurking just out of sight.

I knew I had to take action. I called in a private security firm to ensure my family's safety. They conducted thorough background checks and installed surveillance cameras around our home. Jean was supportive but understandably worried, her eyes reflecting the fear that now haunted our lives.

Despite these precautions, a gnawing anxiety settled in. The letters continued, each one more menacing than the last, detailing my daily routines and mentioning moments I thought were private. "You think you can hide? You're not as clever as you think," one particularly chilling note read.

The tipping point came one evening when I returned home from work. The front door was slightly ajar—a detail that sent alarm bells ringing in my mind. I rushed inside, calling out for Jean and the boys. Panic surged as I moved through the house, finally finding them in the living room, safe but visibly shaken.

"Someone was here," Jean said, her voice trembling. "The cameras… they were disabled."

My heart sank. I felt exposed, vulnerable. This was serious. I contacted the police, but with no concrete evidence, their hands were tied. "We'll keep an eye on your neighbourhood," the officer said, but I could tell he didn't feel optimistic.

The business was at a standstill, and I felt the weight of responsibility pressing down on me. I understood the stakes all too well; with a slew of international consignments due for delivery, maintaining my company's stellar reputation was paramount. Failure to deliver on time could tarnish years of hard-earned trust and credibility in the industry. Clients were depending on me, and the thought of disappointing them was intolerable.

As I leaned back in my chair, a rush of thoughts coursed through my mind. I knew I had to take swift action to resolve the labour strike and ensure the safety of my family.

Just as I was diving into my thoughts, my phone rang, the red light beside the extension one blinking insistently. It was my private line, and I instinctively knew it could be important. I picked up the handset, and Carl's familiar voice greeted me on the other end.

"Hey, Chetan! It's me, Carl," he said, a hint of urgency in his tone. "I need to talk to you about something crucial. I've got a friend who's in a real bind, and I think you're the only one who can help."

My mind raced back to our previous conversation. Carl had mentioned a friend in trouble but hadn't gone into detail at the time. Given the precarious nature of my current situation, I felt a flicker of apprehension, but I couldn't say no to Carl.

"Of course, Carl," I replied, my voice steady despite the chaos surrounding me. "I remember our chat. Bring him over. I'll have security allow you both inside the warehouse and escort you to my office."

I quickly relayed instructions to the security team, ensuring they were ready to receive Carl and his friend. As I hung up, I took a moment to compose myself. While I was deep in my own troubles, I understood the importance of being there for others.

Carl Rebello had been associated with me for the past three years, initially coming on board as a contractor for my company. From the very beginning, he distinguished himself not just through his skills but also through his steadfast loyalty and honest work ethic. Over time, these qualities earned him a place as my trusted confidante.

Our relationship transcended the confines of typical business interactions; we spent countless hours discussing not only strategic initiatives but also life's many complexities. Whether brainstorming ideas for a project or sharing personal experiences, our conversations were marked by a sense of camaraderie and mutual respect. This evolving friendship had created a solid foundation, allowing us to lean on each other in both professional and personal matters.

So, when Carl mentioned that a friend was in dire need of support, I didn't hesitate. I agreed immediately, driven by my trust in Carl and my instinct to help those in need. I understood the importance of lending a hand, especially for someone connected to a friend I respected deeply.

As I prepared to meet Carl and his friend, I felt a mix of anticipation and curiosity. I was eager to hear the details of the situation and find out how I could contribute. Even in my own tumultuous circumstances,

I found solace in the idea of being able to help someone else.

Moments later, the security team ushered Carl and his friend into my office before returning to their posts at the gate. I rose from my chair, extending my hand in greeting as the two men entered. "Welcome! Please, take a seat," I said, gesturing toward the comfortable sofa facing my desk.

As they settled in, I took a moment to study Carl's friend more closely. At first glance, the man seemed familiar, though I couldn't quite place where I might have encountered him before. He exuded a strong presence, standing nearly six feet tall with a well-built physique. Yet, despite his imposing stature, there was a noticeable tension in his demeanour.

I noticed his nervousness; he fidgeted slightly, and his eyes darted around the room as if he were sizing up his surroundings. But it was the scars on his face and hands that truly caught my attention—each mark seemed to tell a story, bearing silent witness to struggles and challenges he had faced in the past. These scars suggested a life lived on the edge, perhaps filled with more hardship than most would encounter.

I realized I still didn't know much about the man sitting across from me—only that he was a friend of Carl from when they were engineering students, and that he was in need of help. Given the pressing issues weighing on my mind, I decided it was best to get straight to the point. "Carl, could you please introduce your friend properly and let's get to the crux of the matter? I'm short on time and have some urgent matters to attend to."

Carl nodded, understanding the urgency of the situation. "Of course, Chetan. This is my friend Aryan. He's been facing some serious challenges lately." He turned to Aryan, encouraging him to speak. "Why don't you tell Chetan what's going on?"

Aryan began by expressing his gratitude for my time. "Thank you for taking the time, Mr. Chetan. It means a lot. Carl and I go way back—buddies from our Engineering college days," he said, a hint of nostalgia in his voice.

As he settled into the conversation, Aryan shared his story. "After finishing my Engineering degree, life took a turn for the worse. I lost my way and succumbed to some poor choices that led me down a dark path. I ended up involved in crime—things I'm not proud of," he confessed, his tone heavy with regret.

I listened intently, sensing the weight of Aryan's past pressing down on him. "I know I made mistakes, and I've paid for them. I spent eight long years in prison, and I've come to terms with my past. Now that my sentence is over, I'm determined to start anew and take care of my family."

He paused for a moment, collecting his thoughts. "But it hasn't been easy. I've been trying to find a respectable job, to rebuild my life, but my history keeps haunting me. No one seems willing to give me a chance. Every door I knock on closes in my face because of my tainted past."

I felt a surge of empathy for Aryan. The journey to redemption was fraught with challenges, and I could see how hard he was trying to forge a new path. "I appreciate your honesty, Aryan. It takes courage to share your story, especially considering the stigma attached to it."

Aryan sat before me, tears welling in his eyes, his hands clasped tightly together in a gesture of supplication. "Chetan," he began, his voice trembling with emotion, "I'm asking you for a chance—an opportunity to live an honourable life. I want to build a career that my family can be proud of, something that will allow me to support them and show them that I've changed."

The weight of his words hung in the air, and I could see the raw vulnerability etched on Aryan's face. I felt a deep sense of compassion welling up inside me as I stared into his painful eyes. I understood all too well the struggles of navigating life's miseries without a safety net or support system.

Taking a deep breath, I nodded slowly, affirming Aryan's plea. "I see how hard you've fought to get here, and I recognize the sincerity in your desire to turn your life around. I promise you this: I will support you in rebuilding your career and getting your life back on track. This is a commitment I'm willing to make."

Aryan's breath caught in his throat, and he blinked away tears as relief flooded his expression. I continued, "I never shy away from a promise. You'll have my backing, but I also need to see your dedication and hard work. This is just the beginning, and it won't be easy. You'll have to prove yourself, but I believe you can do it."

As I spoke, I felt a profound sense of purpose. By extending my support to Aryan, I was not only helping someone in need but also rediscovering my own resilience in the face of adversity. The challenges in my own life—the labour strike, the threats—still loomed large, but in this moment, all that mattered was this stranger sitting in front of me.

The strange thought that I knew this man from somewhere kept gnawing at me, like an itch I couldn't quite scratch. As Aryan spoke about his past and aspirations, my thoughts drifted back, searching for a memory that would connect the dots. There was something about his face, the way he carried himself, that felt eerily familiar.

I glanced at Aryan again, noticing the scars—each one a silent testament to a life lived on the edge. Perhaps it was the intensity in his eyes or the tremor in his voice that stirred a sense of recognition in me. I had encountered many individuals in my line of work, but there was something unique about Aryan, a depth of experience that resonated deeply.

As he detailed his skills and how he could be of use, I found it increasingly difficult to focus on the conversation. Memories flickered in and out of my mind—faces in the crowd, fleeting encounters, perhaps even a news article I'd read long ago. Was it possible I had seen Aryan before, maybe in a different context? Perhaps at an event, or even on the news? My heart raced at the thought; I had always prided myself on being observant, and this was one connection I couldn't afford to overlook.

"Wait," I interrupted gently, causing Aryan to pause mid-sentence. "Have we met before? I mean, somewhere outside of this meeting?"

He looked taken aback for a moment, his brow furrowing as he searched his own memory. "I… I don't know," he admitted slowly, the nervousness creeping back into his demeanour. "Maybe? I've been around quite a bit and have been in the newspapers a few times, obviously for the wrong reasons. But I can't say for sure."

I leaned back, contemplating. "It's just that something about you seems familiar, and I can't quite put my finger on it. Maybe I've seen you at an event? Or perhaps in a different context altogether?"

The room fell silent as we both pondered this possibility. My mind raced, trying to piece together the fragments of recognition. The urgency of our earlier discussion about Aryan's struggles faded slightly as this new mystery took centre stage.

"Whatever the case may be," I finally said, breaking the silence, "I'm here to help you now. But I can't shake the feeling that our paths have crossed before. Let's focus on how we can move forward from here."

As Aryan nodded, I couldn't shake the feeling of intrigue. The familiarity nagged at me, but for now, I pushed it aside, redirecting my energy toward the pressing matter at hand. The conversation resumed, but in the back of my mind, the question lingered—who was this man, really, and how had our lives intersected before?

All this while, Carl smiled, knowing all too well that this was exactly the kind of response Chetan would have. He had anticipated his friend's compassionate nature even before he first broached the topic of helping Aryan. He knew very well that Chetan was in dire straits and that having a strong arm like Aryan would benefit him. Likewise, Chetan was exactly the kind of guy who could get Aryan out of the mess he was in. It was a testament to Chetan's character—always willing to extend a hand to those in need.

I watched as Aryan sat quietly; his gaze locked onto mine. There was something in my eyes that seemed to tug at the edges of his memory. I could see it in the way he furrowed his brow, as if trying to place where he might have seen that mix of kindness and strength before. In that moment, I felt the weight of my own gaze—a reminder of the humanity that binds us all.

Gratitude swelled in him, I could tell, for Carl, who had facilitated this pivotal meeting. Aryan's voice, steadier now, broke the silence. "Thank you, both of you. I can't express how much this means to me. You're giving me a chance to turn my life around, and I promise I won't take it for granted. I'll do anything, and I mean it when I say I'll do absolutely anything necessary to repay your faith."

He stood up, extending his hand toward me. That handshake felt monumental, a significant gesture marking the beginning of a new chapter in his life. I grasped his hand firmly, feeling the weight of mentorship and support coursing between us.

As we shook hands, I felt a warmth envelop him, as if my strength was transferring into his spirit. "Let's make this work," I said, offering him a determined smile.

Hope sparkled in his eyes, and he nodded. In that moment, it felt like a turning point for both of us—a fresh start he had long yearned for. I glanced over at Carl, who was watching with a proud smile, and I sensed that Aryan felt the weight of his past begin to lift, if only slightly.

"Thank you, Carl, for believing in me," Aryan said, turning to his friend. "I couldn't have done this without your support."

Carl shrugged, a humble grin on his face. "You did the hard part by showing up, Aryan. Now it's time to move forward."

I signalled for my front office boy to bring in three cups of coffee, and we settled into a moment of silence, sipping the rich brew. The aroma filled the room, grounding us as we reflected on the weight of our earlier conversation. It was Aryan who finally broke the stillness, but I took the lead.

"The first task I'm assigning to you," I began, shifting my tone to one of authority, "is to get my factory and warehouse running again. You have one week to accomplish this feat." I paused, allowing the gravity of my words to sink in. "Think of this as a test—an evaluation of your skills in getting things done."

Aryan listened intently, nodding as he processed my directive. I continued, "Carl will brief you on everything you need to know about the workers and their union. You'll need to navigate those waters carefully if you want to bring them back to the table. In the meantime, you can make the company quarters here your home. Whatever you need, I'm here for you."

I leaned in slightly, locking eyes with Aryan, my gaze hardening. "But remember, Aryan, I'm desperate for this strike to end. The livelihood of many depends on it. Am I clear?"

I could see the weight of my piercing stare sink in, and Aryan's determination shone through as he replied, "Yes, Chetan. I understand the stakes, and I won't let you down. I'll do everything I can to resolve this issue and get the workers back on track."

I nodded, feeling satisfied with his response. "Good. I need someone who's willing to roll up their sleeves and dig in. This isn't just about negotiations; it's a power struggle that's playing out right now, and I need to win at all costs."

His next words struck a chord with me. "I'm glad you found me worthy of this task, sir. I assure you; I'll leave no stone unturned to end this strike and get everyone back to their work as soon as possible." He paused, his voice steady and resolute. "With the grace of Lord Shiva, I will succeed."

In that moment, I froze. A jolt of recognition shot through me. That phrase echoed in my mind like a familiar song. Memories rushed back—vivid and clear. I recalled a childhood friend who had always said those exact words, a mantra of sorts we'd shared during challenges. "With the grace of Lord Shiva, I will succeed."

Suddenly, everything clicked into place. The familiarity I had sensed in Aryan was rooted in our shared history—a connection spanning years that was now re-emerging in this unexpected context. My heart raced as I processed the revelation. Could this be the same Aryan I had known all those years ago?

"Aryan? Aryan Khan from Bombay?" I asked, my voice low and almost incredulous.

His eyes widened in shock; disbelief etched across his face. How could I possibly know his full name? We had just met, and he had never mentioned it during our conversation. Confusion washed over him as he searched my expression for answers. Slowly, he nodded, still reeling from the unexpected recognition.

"Aryan, it's me, Chetan Verma," I continued, warmth and nostalgia flooding my voice. "Do you remember me? Back from when we were kids?"

A flicker of recognition sparked in his eyes, and I could almost see the memories resurfacing like fragments of a forgotten dream. Images danced in his mind—carefree days spent in our childhood neighbourhood, long afternoons filled with laughter, the sound of a cricket bat striking a ball, and the deep bond of friendship we had once shared.

As the realization settled between us, I felt a mix of emotions. Here we were, two boys who had navigated the ups and downs of life, now standing on the precipice of a new chapter. It felt surreal, and I couldn't help but wonder how we had ended up here, at this moment, after all those years apart.

Carl, who had been sitting quietly all this while, was now completely speechless, taken aback by the sudden turn of events. The revelations unfolding before him felt like a scene from a movie, too surreal to be real. Never in his wildest dreams had he anticipated witnessing such a poignant reunion between Chetan and Aryan.

As he observed the two men, their expressions shifting from shock to recognition to warmth, Carl felt a mixture of emotions swirling inside him. He had known Chetan as a determined and principled leader, someone who cared deeply about those around him. Now, seeing him connect on an emotional level with Aryan—a man who had faced significant struggles—added an entirely new layer to Chetan's character that Carl had not fully appreciated before.

Carl's mind raced as he reflected on the serendipity of the situation. He had introduced Aryan to Chetan, hoping for a chance to help his friend, but he had never imagined that the CEO of one of the largest shipping companies would be someone from a dreaded criminal like Aryan's past. It was as if the universe had conspired to bring them together at this crucial moment. It was literally like a movie scene was playing out in front of his eyes!

Aryan and I were long-lost friends, separated by the relentless passage of time and the unpredictable twists of life. Today, we had unwittingly crossed paths, and it took a few heart-stopping moments for the recognition to sink in. Years had altered our appearances and lives, yet the essence of our friendship lingered just beneath the surface.

It felt like fate had brought us together at a moment when we both needed it most. Aryan was standing at a critical juncture, desperately seeking a chance to rebuild his life after years of hardship. I could see the hope in his eyes, a yearning for someone to look beyond his past and recognize the potential he had to contribute meaningfully to society.

On the flip side, I was grappling with my own pressing challenges. My company, a testament to years of hard work and dedication, was teetering on the brink due to the ongoing strike. The stakes were high, threatening not just my livelihood but the safety of my family and myself.

Call it destiny, fate, or whatever you wish; this reunion felt like our Karma. In that moment, I realized that our lives had intertwined once more, and perhaps, together, we could navigate the complexities ahead.

CHAPTER 2
THEIR CHILDHOOD

Aryan and I had always been friends for as long as I could remember. Back in the mid-sixties, we spent our days playing together, our laughter echoing through the streets of our neighbourhood. We were inseparable, bound by a friendship that felt destined to last forever.

Aryan's father was an accomplished engineer, an IIT alumnus renowned for his innovative designs and influential projects. He was immensely successful in his career, well-respected in society, and a figure of admiration for many in our community.

My father, on the other hand, was a dedicated defence personnel, known for his impeccable service record and unwavering commitment to his country. His discipline was legendary; he held himself and our family to the highest standards. Though Aryan and I came from vastly different backgrounds, we shared one significant trait: both our fathers were strict disciplinarians.

For my father, being a disciplinarian was a lifestyle. He believed that structure and routine were essential to personal development, instilling in me the importance of hard work, punctuality, and respect for authority. Every evening, I found myself engaged in various activities designed to foster responsibility—whether it was studying, practicing sports, or contributing to household chores. It was a rigorous upbringing, but one that prepared me for the challenges ahead.

In contrast, Aryan's father held a different philosophy. He believed that the only recipe for success was a singular focus on one's goals, free from unnecessary distractions. This relentless pursuit of excellence became Aryan's way of life, and I watched as he strived to achieve the highest grades in school and excel in extracurricular activities. His father's drive for achievement pushed him to dedicate countless hours to his studies, often sacrificing playtime to ensure he stayed ahead.

But it was the aggression behind Aryan's father's approach that truly shocked me. The pressure to conform to such high standards came at a cost—there were times when Aryan returned home with bruises on his hands and legs for stepping out of line

I was a year senior to Aryan at school, and our friendship blossomed as we navigated the ups and downs of childhood together. I found myself taking on a protective role, looking after my younger friend with a sense of responsibility that felt completely natural. Whether it involved helping Aryan with his homework, guiding him through challenging subjects, or shielding him from bullies on the playground, I was always there— a steadfast presence in his life.

I prided myself on knowing when to offer encouragement and when to step in, ensuring Aryan felt supported in every endeavour. My confidence and leadership qualities shone through, and I could see the admiration in his eyes. It felt as if I naturally filled the role of an elder brother, not just a friend.

In turn, Aryan looked up to me with unwavering admiration. He was captivated by my ability to navigate challenges with poise and determination, traits that seemed effortless to me but meant the world to him. Aryan made it a point to be around me whenever he could—during lunch breaks, after school activities, or just hanging out on weekends. We were virtually inseparable, forming a bond that felt both comforting and empowering.

Once, when we were around ten years old, I found myself caught up in a playful cricket match in our bustling colony. The sun was shining, laughter filled the air, and the thrill of the game was electric. In a moment of excitement, I swung my bat with all my might, sending the cricket ball soaring through the sky. To my horror, it crashed through the window panes of a grumpy auntie's house, shattering the peacefulness of the afternoon.

Panic erupted as all the kids, myself included, took off running, our hearts racing at the thought of the trouble we'd landed in. We darted away from the scene, laughter morphing into fearful giggles as we fled, leaving the chaos behind us. But Aryan was a moment too late to escape; I noticed him hesitate, realizing he had left his prized bat and stumps behind in the frenzy.

With a sigh of resignation, he turned back to retrieve his gear, knowing he had to face the music

That evening, the repercussions came crashing down. The old lady, furious and indignant, marched over to Aryan's house and unleashed a torrent of complaints to his father. Aryan's heart sank as he listened to her accusations, knowing he would soon be in trouble. When his father learned of the incident, he was not amused. In a stern voice, he reprimanded Aryan, who felt the weight of his father's disappointment heavy on his shoulders. He received a thorough scolding that turned into a punishment he wouldn't soon forget.

But what weighed most heavily on Aryan's heart wasn't the punishment he received; it was the thought of Chetan facing the consequences alone. Despite his own discomfort, Aryan couldn't bring himself to let his friend take the blame for something that had been an accident—albeit a clumsy one. He could have easily pointed fingers and absolved himself of any responsibility, but that wasn't his character. He had always believed in loyalty and friendship, and in that moment, it was probably clear to him that he would protect me at all costs.

As Aryan sat in his room that night, nursing the sting of his father's reprimand, he made a silent vow. He would never let me suffer alone; our friendship meant too much to him. While the punishment was harsh, Aryan felt a sense of pride in his decision to shield his friend. He knew that true friendship sometimes required sacrifices, and he was willing to bear the brunt of the consequences for my sake.

Another time, when we were in their early teens, Aryan found himself drawn into a world he wasn't ready for. Influenced by some of the older boys in their colony, he picked up the habit of smoking occasional cigarettes, convinced that it made him look cool and grown-up. The allure of rebellion and acceptance clouded his judgment, and for a while, he thought he was fitting in.

However, I soon discovered Aryan's secret. A surge of anger mixed with concern coursed through me. Knowing that Aryan was simply trying to find his place in the world, I couldn't stand by and watch as he made choices that could lead to harm. With a firm resolve, I sought out the elder boy who had introduced Aryan to smoking.

Confronting him, I felt a fierce intensity surge within me. I warned the boy of dire consequences if I ever saw him near Aryan again. "You think you're cool, messing with kids who don't know any better? Stay away from him, or you'll regret it," I declared, my voice steady but laced with barely contained fury.

The elder boy, taken aback by my fierce loyalty and the intensity of my emotions, felt his bravado wane. I could see the colour drain from his face as he realized he had underestimated my protective instincts. The threat hung in the air, palpable and charged.

"Okay, okay! I'll back off!" he stammered, his confidence evaporating. With that hurried promise, he retreated, casting a wary glance over his shoulder as he left.

Later that day, Aryan, feeling both ashamed and relieved, approached Chetan. "I'm sorry," he said, his voice barely above a whisper. He could hardly meet my eyes, overwhelmed by guilt for putting his friend in such a position. "I didn't mean to worry you."

Without hesitation, I pulled Aryan into a tight embrace. "I just want you to be safe, man. You're my best friend. I care about you too much to let you make those kinds of choices," I said, my voice softer now, filled with genuine concern.

"I promise I won't do it again. I swear," he said, returning my hug with an intensity that spoke volumes about his remorse. In that moment, I felt our bond solidify even further; it was a powerful reminder of how far I was willing to go to protect him.

Because of the strong friendship Aryan and I shared, our families formed a remarkable bond as well. The warmth and affection between our two households blossomed effortlessly. Our parents appreciated the friendship we had cultivated, recognizing it as a source of joy and support for both of us.

We often found ourselves invited to each other's homes, where the atmosphere was always filled with laughter and stories. Family dinners became a cherished tradition—each gathering an opportunity for our parents to connect over shared interests while Aryan and I played and reminisced about our adventures. The tables would be laden with delicious home-cooked meals, and the sound of clinking dishes mingled with the joyful chatter in the house.

Additionally, our families frequently went on vacations together, transforming weekends into unforgettable getaways filled with fun and exploration. Whether it was a trip to the nearby hills, a beach resort, or a simple camping excursion, these shared experiences forged lasting memories for us all. Aryan and I would spend hours hiking, swimming, and playing games, our laughter echoing through the woods or along the shoreline. Meanwhile, our parents enjoyed each other's company, often reminiscing about their own childhoods and laughing at our antics.

On one such camping trip near a hillside on the outskirts of town, our friendship faced another trial.

One sweltering summer afternoon, the two of us decided to explore the nearby woods, a place filled with tall trees, winding trails, and the promise of adventure. We had built a makeshift fort there—a hideout where we could escape the world and be just kids. As we ventured deeper into the woods, our laughter echoed among the trees, but soon we stumbled upon a clearing that looked different from our usual playground. Intrigued, we moved closer, only to find a group of older boys gathered around a small fire.

"What do you want?" one of them sneered as Aryan and I approached.

"This is our spot." Aryan, always the brave one, puffed up his chest. "We just wanted to check it out. We're not bothering anyone."

The older boys exchanged glances, and I felt a knot tightening in my stomach. One of them, a tall kid with a cocky grin, stepped forward. "Well, now you are. Why don't you show us what you've got?".

I instinctively stepped in front of Aryan. "We don't want any trouble. Just let us go back to our fort." But the bully wasn't having it. "You think you're tough because you can talk back? Prove it!" With a swift motion, he shoved me, sending me stumbling backward. Aryan's eyes widened in fear, and he grabbed my arm. "Let's just go, Chetan," he urged, his voice trembling.

I hesitated, feeling the pressure of Aryan's hand on my arm. But the thought of backing down in front of my friend felt unbearable. "No. I'm not afraid of you," I said defiantly, looking the bully in the eye.

The confrontation escalated quickly. The bully's friends closed in, and before I could react, they began taunting me, shoving me back and forth. I felt the heat rising in his chest, fuelled by a mix of anger and fear for

Aryan's safety. I couldn't let them intimidate him or Aryan. Suddenly, the bully swung a punch, catching me squarely in the jaw. Pain shot through me, but I refused to fall. Instead, I swung back, landing a punch that surprised both the bully and myself.

The other boys shouted, egging their friend on, and chaos erupted as they all joined in. In the midst of the fight, I felt a surge of adrenaline. I fought back fiercely, but the odds were stacked heavily against me. Aryan, frozen in shock, watched as I was knocked to the ground. Just when it seemed all was lost, something snapped inside Aryan.

"Stop it!" Aryan yelled, charging forward. He didn't care about the risk; he couldn't watch me get hurt, I suppose. He grabbed a nearby stick and swung it at the nearest bully, surprising everyone, including me. "Get away from my friend!" Aryan shouted, his voice echoing with a strength I didn't know he had.

The older boys paused, taken aback by Aryan's unexpected bravery. I, seeing Aryan stand up for me once again, felt a rush of gratitude and pride.

"You're not alone, Chetan!" Aryan shouted again, rallying his courage. With Aryan's intervention, the tide began to turn. The older boys, realizing they were now facing two determined kids instead of one, began to lose their confidence.

Just then, the sound of an adult's voice came from the direction of the main path. "What's going on here?" A park ranger had spotted the commotion and was making his way toward us. The bullies exchanged nervous glances and, sensing they were about to get caught, quickly scattered into the woods. Aryan and I stood panting, adrenaline coursing through our veins, hearts racing.

"Are you okay?" Aryan asked, concern flooding his voice as he helped me to my feet. I wiped the dirt from my clothes, a smile breaking through despite the bruises.

"Yeah, thanks to you. I didn't think you'd jump in like that" I said.

"I couldn't let them hurt you," Aryan replied, relief washing over him. "We're in this together, right?"

"Always," I affirmed, feeling our deep bond of friendship strengthening even further. The drama of the day had perfectly described our friendship; one built on loyalty, bravery, and the unshakeable understanding that we would always stand up for each other—no matter what.

As the years rolled on, it seemed as though Aryan and I were destined to be inseparable for life.

However, fate had something else in store for us. Aryan's father received a job offer in another city that he couldn't refuse, and that decision altered the course of our lives. It was a bitter moment overshadowed by the sadness of impending separation. In those days before mobile phones and emails, the world felt much larger, and distances seemed insurmountable. The internet revolution was still a distant dream, and our communication was limited to letters or occasional landline calls. Eventually, even these ended.

As we completed our school education, life took us in divergent directions. I stayed in our hometown, immersing myself in my studies and nurturing the ambitions my parents had instilled in me. Each day felt like a careful balancing act, as I tried to honour their dreams while grappling with my own aspirations. Aryan, however, faced a different challenge. He was thrust into a new city, a new school, and a whirlwind of unfamiliar faces.

The abruptness of our separation left both of us heartbroken; it was as if a vital piece of my soul had been severed. The laughter we had shared, the secrets whispered under the stars, and the dreams we'd woven together felt like distant echoes now. I often found myself staring at old photographs, reminiscing about the carefree days when everything seemed possible.

In his new environment, Aryan had to adapt quickly, making new friends and forging a new identity. I wondered if he ever felt the same pang of loss that I did, or if he had managed to immerse himself fully in his new life. As the months turned into years, I would continue thinking about him.

Despite the miles between us, I held onto the hope that our paths would cross again, that we'd find our way back to each other amid the chaos of our new lives. After all, some connections are too deep to be truly severed; they simply lie dormant, waiting for the right moment to reignite.

Friendship loss is often deep and confusing, and ours was no exception. There was no magic band-aid or waving of a wand that could take away the pain of losing a cherished bond. As the days turned into weeks and weeks into months, we tried to cope with the void left in our hearts. We had once spent most of the day together, but now we were alone, staring at a world that felt emptier without each other.

The emotional scars ran deep. I found it challenging to forge new friendships, often comparing everyone to Aryan, holding them up to the impossible standard set by our earlier bond. Whenever I encountered someone new, the shadows of our lost friendship crept in, leading to a lingering sense of disappointment. No one seemed to measure up; there was always that unshakeable feeling that something vital was missing.

As far as Aryan and I were concerned, ours was the ultimate friendship. We were the often quoted 'Brothers of different mothers.' And brothers couldn't be separated forever. No, we would definitely meet again, and in the meantime, we would have to fulfil our *Karma*.

CHAPTER 3
CHETAN'S PATH

I joined college with a mix of excitement and determination, envisioning a bright future ahead. As the semester progressed, my efforts in academics began to pay off. I aced my exams, earning high grades and academic recognition. But it wasn't just academics where I thrived. I also sought opportunities beyond the classroom. I joined the student council, where I advocated for student concerns and organized events. Leading a team of passionate students was a challenge, but it taught me invaluable lessons in leadership and collaboration. Each event we organized brought us closer, strengthening the sense of community on campus.

One of my proudest moments came when I was elected as the vice president of the student government. Graduation day arrived, and the air was filled with a mix of excitement and nostalgia. As I walked across the stage to receive my diploma, I reflected on my journey—how I had grown from a nervous freshman to a confident, capable young adult. The challenges I faced, and the experiences I gained had shaped me in ways I could never have imagined.

As I tossed my cap into the air, I felt an overwhelming sense of gratitude. College had not just been about excelling in my studies; it had been about discovering myself. I left college ready to embrace whatever came next, knowing that I was equipped with the skills and resilience to overcome any difficulties that lay ahead.

Upon completing my graduation, I dove headfirst into the job market, eager to find a career that matched my skills and aspirations. However, this phase turned out to be a real struggle for me. The bustling streets of Mumbai became both my playground and battleground as I spent countless days job hunting, fuelled by a relentless drive to succeed.

Armed with my resume and firm resolve, I walked over fifty kilometres a day, traversing the city from one end to the other in search of opportunities. Each step felt heavy, and with barely half a meal to sustain me, exhaustion began to take its toll. Despite my tenacity, results were elusive. Rejection after rejection piled up, each one adding another layer to my mounting frustration.

What compounded my struggles was the fact that my father was influential and well-connected in the industry. Securing a good job opportunity for me would have been nothing more than a cakewalk for him. Yet, in a bewildering move, he firmly refused to help. He believed that the best way for me to grow was to experience hardship first hand—to become an idealistic self-made man. This stubborn belief, rooted in the values he held dear, felt both unrealistic and harsh to me.

To add salt to the wounds, the landscape of job hunting in India during those days was rife with connections and money. Almost anything could be done with the right contacts, and it wasn't uncommon for positions to be filled through personal recommendations or financial incentives. I couldn't help but feel the irony of my situation: while many around me leveraged connections to secure their futures, I was bound by my father's ideals. His way of helping me was ironically through not helping, believing that I needed to succeed without money or connections—a notion that felt laughable in those times.

However, this struggle only fuelled the fire of my resolve. Each setback stoked my desire to succeed, and I became even more determined to prove my worth—not just to my father, but to myself. I kept reminding myself that giving up was simply not an option. I had faced challenges before and emerged stronger; this was just another test of my character. "I have to soldier on," I told myself, envisioning my ultimate destiny just within reach.

Days turned into weeks, and as I continued to navigate the bustling streets of Mumbai, I remained steadfast in my belief that opportunity would eventually knock. My spirit was unyielding, a testament to my steely resolve and character.

And speaking of soldiering on, I eventually caught a break that would change the trajectory of my career: I received an offer to join the Navy.

The tough times I had already experienced and conquered at such a young age forged me into a resilient and determined individual. Each challenge became a stepping stone, moulding my character and instilling a sense of toughness that would define my approach to life. Beneath this exterior, however, lay a well of latent anger and frustration, much of it stemming from my father's staunch refusal to offer support during a critical time in my life. This internal struggle fuelled my relentless pursuit of success, driving me to prove myself at every turn.

In the Navy, I found a world that not only tested my mettle but also provided an outlet for my ambitions. I threw myself into my training, excelling in both physical and mental challenges. My discipline and work ethic set me apart from my comrades. Where others might falter, I persevered, driven by a desire to transform my pain into power and to make a name for myself.

As I navigated through various roles and responsibilities, I quickly outshone my peers in almost every aspect. Whether it was strategic planning, leadership skills, or physical endurance, I consistently set a high standard. My dedication didn't go unnoticed; I garnered the respect and admiration of my superiors and colleagues alike. My ability to rise to challenges with grace and determination became my trademark, and I embraced each new opportunity as a chance to demonstrate my capabilities.

Within no time, at the remarkably young age of twenty-six, I achieved a milestone that few could even dream of: I became the youngest Captain in the Navy's history! The moment I received that news, a wave of exhilaration washed over me, accompanied by an undeniable sense of pride. It wasn't just a title; it was a testament to my unwavering determination and the countless sacrifices I had made along the way.

After a while, I decided it was time to leave the Navy and explore the vast ocean of opportunities in the corporate world, particularly in shipping companies. My experiences in the Navy had provided me with invaluable skills and a disciplined mindset, but I felt a compelling urge to apply my talents in a different arena—one that offered more growth opportunities and a wider horizon for my ambitious spirit.

The corporate business world was teeming with possibilities, and I was eager to dive in. I understood that while the Navy had shaped me into a strong leader, the corporate sector would allow me to leverage that leadership in new and innovative ways. With a reputation for excellence and a record of achievement, I believed I could make a significant impact in the shipping industry, where my passion for logistics and operations could truly flourish.

I envisioned myself not just as a participant in this new realm, but as a leader who could innovate and drive change. The corporate environment felt like a blank canvas, waiting for my brush strokes to paint a new picture of success. I wanted to create a legacy that combined my navy background with entrepreneurial spirit—where discipline met creativity, and strategy blended with passion.

Ambition was my proverbial middle name, and I was ready for a new adventure.

I dedicated myself wholeheartedly to my work, pouring in tireless efforts that yielded outstanding results. Each late night and early morning added another layer to my reputation, and my commitment and drive didn't go unnoticed. Before long, I established myself as a top-notch achiever in the corporate landscape, recognized not just for my results but for my leadership style—a blend of discipline and innovation, much like my time in the Navy.

By the age of thirty-six, I found myself at the helm of a large shipping company as its Chief Executive Officer—a remarkable feat that many could only dream of. The position came with its challenges, but I thrived in the high-pressure environment.

This wasn't merely a title; it was another feather in my cap, an addition to the growing portfolio of achievements that marked my career. I didn't seek validation, but I had set very high standards for myself and was determined to meet them with grit and determination. And achieve them I did! I never wanted to struggle again. Work became my full-time hobby, and success became my mantra.

I found myself unavoidably traversing the globe for my profession, embarking on journeys that took me to a vast array of destinations. My globe-trotting adventures led me to the bustling streets of cosmopolitan cities like New York, London, and Tokyo, where I mingled with influential business leaders, attended high-stakes meetings, and immersed myself in the vibrant cultures. The energy of these cities fuelled my ambition, each skyline a testament to human ingenuity and the relentless pursuit of success.

At the same time, I ventured into isolated countryside locations, where the simplicity of life presented its own unique challenges and rewards. Here, in remote villages, I witnessed the stark contrast of wealth and poverty, the resilience of communities that thrived despite their hardships. These experiences grounded me, reminding me of the broader impact of our corporate decisions. In every conversation, whether in a high-rise boardroom or a small-town café, I sought to understand the human stories behind the numbers, believing that true leadership involved a balance of profit and purpose.

Every destination left its mark on me. The skyscrapers of New York taught me ambition, while the serene landscapes of rural India instilled a sense of gratitude. Each journey shaped my worldview, expanding my understanding of global markets while deepening my appreciation for the local nuances that drive them.

Through this traveling and working amidst different countries and cultures, my management and administrative skills grew ten-fold. I became a master at closing huge deals, navigating intricate negotiations, and handling even the pettiest of issues with finesse. Every encounter was an opportunity to refine my approach, whether it was securing a multi-million-dollar contract in a high-stakes boardroom or resolving a logistical hiccup in a small port town.

I learned to treat every challenge as a stepping stone to greener pastures beyond them.

Speaking of greener pastures, my life took a delightful turn during one of my overseas postings, where I met Jean. I remember that week in London vividly. The conference was intense, filled with back-to-back meetings and strategy sessions. But everything changed the moment Jean walked into the conference room. I still can't explain it, but there was something about her—her bright eyes, the way she carried herself with confidence. She just had this energy that drew me in.

As we moved through the agenda, I found myself stealing glances at her. Every time our eyes met;

it felt like a spark ignited between us. The chemistry was undeniable. When the meeting wrapped up, I knew I had to act. My heart raced as I approached her, feeling a mix of excitement and nervousness. "How about a cup of coffee?" I asked, hoping she'd say yes.

To my delight, she smiled brightly and agreed, her eyes sparkling with enthusiasm. We wandered to a cosy café nearby, a hidden gem known for its rich coffee and warm ambiance. As we settled into a corner table, my initial nervousness began to fade, replaced by a comfortable familiarity that felt almost magical.

Our conversation flowed effortlessly, covering a multitude of topics. We shared stories from our childhoods, laughing about the innocence of youth and the mischief we got into. Jean recounted a particularly amusing incident involving her attempt to bake cookies for her family, which had turned into a kitchen disaster. I shared my own tales of adventure and mischief, regaling her with anecdotes of my struggles and triumphs in the corporate world. She seemed particularly impressed with my stint in the Navy. I was even more impressed with the dimples on her face.

As the hours passed, we delved deeper into more personal subjects—discussing our families, dreams, and aspirations. I admired Jean's ambition; she spoke passionately about her goals and the impact she wanted to make in the business world. She seemed as intelligent as she was beautiful; and that was probably a reason that drew me towards her. I found himself captivated by her vision, her intelligence, and the way she expressed her thoughts with such clarity. In return, I opened up about my own journey, revealing the challenges I had overcome and my relentless pursuit of success. I explained to her how being a workaholic in my pursuit for success was vital to me, and she seemed to understand.

Time slipped away unnoticed, and before we knew it, the café was preparing to close for the night. I didn't want the evening to end, so I suggested we continue our conversation over dinner. Jean's eyes lit up at the idea, and we quickly made our way to a nearby restaurant renowned for its delightful cuisine.

The atmosphere at dinner felt even more intimate. We indulged in delicious dishes, sharing our favourite cuisines and hobbies—my love for fitness and running, her passion for painting. Each revelation drew us closer; there were no awkward silences or forced conversations. Instead, we filled the air with laughter, exchanged shared glances, and revelled in each other's company. She looked even prettier when a strand of hair came down her face, and it took all my will power to resist the urge to gently put it back. Sigh! Being attracted to someone is as silly as it is magical.

By the time the night wrapped up, the sky was adorned with a blanket of stars, twinkling like diamonds. I walked Jean to her doorstep, both of us reluctant to say goodbye. As we reached her front door, I took her hand in mine, our fingers intertwining naturally, as if they had always belonged together.

"Can we do this again tomorrow?" I asked, my voice barely above a whisper, hoping she could sense the sincerity in my tone.

Her face lit up with a radiant smile, her excitement palpable. "Absolutely," she replied, her eyes shimmering with anticipation.

We lingered for a while, staring into each other's eyes, and savouring the moment. It felt like the world around us had faded away. Then, leaning in, I gently kissed her cheek—I usually am not so confident, however what is more important, is that she smiled. When I finally left, I couldn't shake the feeling that this was just the beginning of something truly special.

As I walked back to my hotel, I felt lighter than air, the weight of my professional struggles momentarily forgotten. My mind was filled with thoughts of Jean—our laughter, our conversations, and that undeniable spark that ignited between us. Little did I know, this meeting was just the beginning. It would not only lead to a casual romance but also mark a new chapter in my life, igniting feelings within me I didn't know existed. The excitement of what lay ahead sent a thrill through me, and for the first time in a long while, I felt like a young boy again, grinning to myself.

The following days turned into a whirlwind of coffee dates, dinners, and explorations around London. With each meeting, we got closer to each other. Every single time that one of us found time, we invariably called up the other and asked if we could meet. If I called up Jean to check if she wanted to catch up for a quick breakfast at the café before work, she called me to ask if I wanted to go see a movie in the evening. I found myself captivated by Jean's wit and charm. Each laugh we shared felt like a delightful surprise, and I could see how much she admired my ambition and determination.

We explored the city together, visiting iconic landmarks and strolling through lush parks, indulging in the local cuisine that felt like an adventure in itself. Every moment was a discovery, each conversation peeling back new layers of our personalities. I found myself smiling more often than I have ever done in my life; most of the times, for absolutely no reason.

A few months passed, and I found myself falling deeply in love with Jean. She had become not just my confidante but also my greatest supporter, always believing in me even when I doubted myself. I loved how she would listen patiently to my long-winded stories, often teasing me about my tendency to go on and on. And there was something serene about watching her peaceful face when she was engrossed in a book—it made me realize how much I enjoyed just being around her.

We complemented each other to an extent that people around us often commented how perfect they are together. One evening, under the soft glow of fairy lights in a cozy restaurant, I decided it was time to take our relationship to the next level.

As we finished dinner, I took a deep breath, my heart pounding with anticipation. "Jean, I've never felt this way about anyone before. You've changed my life in ways I never thought possible. I can't imagine my future without you," I began, my voice steady but filled with emotion.

I could see the surprise in her eyes, the joy blooming on her face as she absorbed my words. The moment hung in the air, charged with anticipation of what was going to happen next. I felt a rush of vulnerability, but also an overwhelming sense of certainty. She was the one I wanted to share my life with, and I hoped she felt the same way.

Jean's eyes widened, a mix of surprise and joy illuminating her face, when I reached into my pocket and pulled out a small velvet box.

"Will you marry me?" I asked, opening the box to reveal a stunning ring that sparkled like the moments we had shared together.

Tears welled up in Jean's eyes as she gasped, her hand instinctively flying to her mouth. "Oh, Chetan!" she exclaimed, her voice a mix of disbelief and joy. "Yes! Yes, of course, I will!"

In that moment, time seemed to stand still. The restaurant around us faded away, the clinking of cutlery and the murmur of conversations drowned out by the heartbeat of our connection. All that mattered was us. We embraced tightly, the warmth of our love wrapping around us like a comforting blanket, shielding us from the chaos of the world outside.

I could hardly believe this dream was coming true. The journey from that fateful meeting in the conference room to this moment had been nothing short of magical. Each twist and turn had woven a tapestry of experiences—some challenging, some exhilarating—that led us to this very instant. It felt as if the universe had conspired to bring me the happiness I had always desired, yet seldom received in my life.

As we celebrated our engagement and began planning our future together, I couldn't help but reflect on how far I had come—from a young man striving for success to someone ready to build a life filled with love and partnership. With Jean by my side, I felt an unwavering confidence that we could face any challenge that lay ahead, hand in hand.

Within just six months of our first date, Jean and I decided to marry in a small yet intimate ceremony, surrounded by our closest family and friends. The event took place in a charming garden, a hidden gem adorned with fairy lights and blooming flowers, perfectly reflecting the enchantment of our journey together.

As the sun dipped below the horizon, casting a warm golden glow over everything, I felt a rush of emotion. The air was thick with the sweet scent of jasmine, mingling with the laughter of our loved ones, creating an atmosphere that felt almost magical. Each moment was alive, crackling with energy as if the universe itself was celebrating our love.

When Jean walked down the aisle, time stood still. She was breath taking in her simple yet elegant dress, her smile radiant, illuminating the gathering like a beacon. The gentle breeze tousled her hair, and as our eyes locked, the world around us faded away. I could hardly breathe, overwhelmed by the sheer beauty of the moment and the realization that this was my future standing before me.

As we exchanged vows, the soft rustle of leaves whispered secrets of love, and the gentle chirping of birds sang a melody just for us. I promised to cherish her, to be her anchor in stormy seas, and to face life's challenges together. Every word was a sacred vow, a binding thread that wove our hearts together.

My friends from work mingled seamlessly with Jean's family, creating a vibrant tapestry of laughter and joy that filled the air. Conversations flowed effortlessly, blending stories of our lives into a harmonious melody of love and camaraderie. It became clear to everyone just how deeply in love we were. The energy in the garden was electric, a tangible force that seemed to draw everyone closer. Eyes glistened with tears of happiness, and smiles radiated warmth, enveloping us in a cocoon of shared joy. Each heartfelt word we spoke resonated with our guests, who were captivated by the moment, fully immersed in the beauty of our union.

As I gazed into Jean's eyes, I could see our dreams reflected back at me—an entire future filled with love, adventure, and unwavering support. The gentle rustle of the leaves echoed our promises, whispering their approval as if nature itself rejoiced in our love. The sun dipped lower, casting a golden hue over everything, making it feel like time had paused just for us.

In that sacred moment, surrounded by our loved ones, I knew this was more than just a wedding; it was the beginning of a lifelong journey together. Our hearts beat in sync, each promise solidifying the foundation of our shared life, and the world around us faded into a blissful haze, leaving only the two of us, bound by love and hope for the future.

After our wedding, Jean made the brave decision to quit her job. With the frequency of my international transfers, we both knew our family would be constantly on the move, navigating new cities and cultures together. Embracing her new role as a homemaker, she approached it with a blend of enthusiasm and grace, ready to build a home wherever we landed.

The transition wasn't without its challenges; there were moments of doubt and adjustment as she navigated this new chapter. Yet, she found profound fulfilment in creating a loving and nurturing environment for our family. Every meal she prepared, every corner she decorated, and every routine she established became a testament to her dedication.

We reasoned that my earnings were more than enough to ensure a comfortable life for us, allowing Jean to focus on what truly mattered—crafting a sanctuary filled with warmth and love. She turned our temporary houses into homes, infusing them with her spirit and style, making each place feel uniquely ours.

In the midst of our whirlwind lifestyle, Jean became the anchor, the one who kept us grounded. I would come home after long trips, weary from meetings and travels, only to be rejuvenated by the cozy embrace of our home and the delightful aroma of her cooking. Her laughter echoed through the halls, creating a haven that felt like a refuge from the world outside.

As we settled into our new routines, I realized how lucky I was to have someone so dedicated by my side. Jean's commitment to our family was evident in every detail, and her ability to adapt to our ever-changing life only deepened my admiration for her.

In the following years, our lives were blessed with the arrival of two beautiful baby boys, born within just four years of each other. Each child brought a whirlwind of energy and laughter, filling our home with an abundance of love and joy that felt almost magical.

Jean embraced motherhood with a passion that was truly inspiring. She relished every moment spent with our little ones, her laughter mingling with theirs as they explored the world together. The chaos of toddlerhood became a symphony she conducted with grace—playdates were expertly organized, and family outings were meticulously planned, each adventure woven into the fabric of our daily lives.

By God's grace, we were soon blessed with our third son. I often marvelled at how perfect our life had become. Our three sons made our family complete, filling every corner of our home with their infectious energy and boundless curiosity. Jean and I cherished these moments, naming our three beautiful boys Mark, Matthew, and Ronny.

With each passing day, I found myself falling deeper in love with the life we were building together. Watching Jean nurture our children, witnessing her laughter echo through our home, and seeing the boys' bond as brothers filled me with an indescribable happiness. This was all I had ever wanted—a family brimming with love, laughter, and a sense of belonging. Together, we were crafting memories that would last a lifetime, and I couldn't have dreamed of a better life.

Driven by the same ambition that had propelled me through my career, I threw myself into my role as CEO, navigating the complexities of the shipping industry with a fervour that matched my early days in the Navy. Each day brought its own set of challenges, but I tackled them head-on, fuelled by the desire to provide for my family and create a life filled with comfort and opportunity.

As I thrived in my position, the fruits of my labour began to manifest in the lives of Jean and our sons. I ensured they enjoyed the luxuries that came with my success—sun-soaked vacations, beautifully crafted homes, and experiences that would enrich their lives. I watched with pride as my boys explored their passions, encouraged by a mother who poured her heart into nurturing their dreams.

Every achievement at work felt like a stepping stone toward a brighter future for them. With each deal closed, each challenge overcome, my determination deepened.

Our home transformed into a haven of warmth and laughter; its walls adorned with photographs that captured the essence of our happiest moments together. Each image told a story—a family vacation at the beach with sun-kissed smiles, birthday celebrations overflowing with joy, and quiet evenings filled with shared laughter.

I made it a priority to be present for every milestone, whether it was Matthew taking his first steps or Mark scoring a goal in his soccer game. Balancing the relentless demands of my career with my role as a devoted husband and father was no easy feat, but I embraced it wholeheartedly. The late nights at the office and the stress of navigating the corporate landscape faded into the background as soon as I crossed the threshold of our home.

Each evening spent with Jean and our boys became a sacred ritual, a reminder of why I worked so hard in the first place.

My work was flourishing as the shipping company expanded its operations and gained attention in the industry. My relentless dedication and innovative strategies yielded impressive profits and a burgeoning reputation. Yet, with success came the inevitable complexities of corporate life, including a mix of friends and foes.

While I developed valuable relationships with colleagues and industry peers, I also attracted a growing list of enemies. Some of these individuals were directly linked to the communities affected by my company's expansion—people who felt their lives had been disrupted or marginalized by our operations.

As our shipping routes expanded and new ports were built, there were voices of dissent emerging from local activists and community leaders. They challenged the environmental impact of our projects, raising concerns about pollution and displacement. I understood their frustrations; after all, every business decision rippled through the lives of ordinary people. I was determined to address their concerns head-on, believing that a responsible company should not only thrive but also uplift the communities it touched.

Despite my efforts to engage with these groups and seek common ground, there were those who saw my rise as a direct threat to their power or livelihood.

The foreign nature of the company's operations only intensified local tensions. Many villagers felt marginalized and displaced, having seen their lands taken over for corporate development. Their grievances were fuelled by a deep-seated belief that they had been overlooked and undervalued in the name of progress. Protests erupted, ranging from peaceful demonstrations to hostile confrontations, aimed directly at the company and, by extension, at me.

The most alarming aspect of this unrest was the life threats that began to surface. Anonymous notes slipped under my office door, menacing phone calls late at night, and the occasional graffiti on the walls of our facilities served as constant reminders of the growing animosity. I was acutely aware that these threats weren't just aimed at me; they extended to my family as well, adding a layer of stress that gnawed at my peace of mind.

Around that time, one of my contractors named Carl, who coincidentally was also a Navy veteran but served as an engineer, approached me with a peculiar request. He mentioned there was someone who needed help, someone who could potentially be beneficial to the company down the line. However, he didn't provide any specific details—no name, no background, nothing.

Because of the early struggles I faced, where I literally had no assistance from anyone—especially my father—I subconsciously made it my mission to help anyone I could whenever I came across someone in need, especially friends. Those challenges had shaped me profoundly, instilling in me a deep sense of empathy and a desire to uplift others.

I was so affected by the hardships I endured that I made a solemn vow: once I got married and had children, they would never face even the minutest difficulties I had experienced. I envisioned a life for them filled with comfort and security, one where they could chase their passions without the burdens of financial strain or uncertainty. Family meant everything to me, and I was determined that my loved ones would never have to relive the struggles of my past.

Hence, I immediately asked Carl to bring his friend for a meeting, where I would try to help him as best as I could.

This is what resulted in that fateful morning, where I was re-united with Aryan.

CHAPTER 4
ARYAN'S PATH

After moving from his childhood home and being separated from his friends, including me, Aryan immersed himself in his college education. He was a dedicated student, following in his father's footsteps to become an engineer. His hard work paid off when he secured a position in the aviation industry as ground staff, a role that seemed like a promising start.

However, as he settled into this new chapter, Aryan quickly discovered the harsh realities of the corporate world. The environment was rife with favouritism and nepotism—practices he had only heard about in whispers, but never truly understood until now. Despite his diligence and commitment, he found himself overshadowed by colleagues who benefited from connections that opened doors, regardless of their actual qualifications.

Every day, Aryan witnessed the inequities of the system, watching as less qualified individuals were promoted simply because of who they knew, while he remained stuck in the shadows, his efforts seemingly unrecognized. The frustration began to gnaw at him. He had always been ambitious, driven by the desire to excel, but this new reality felt like a betrayal of his values.

He struggled with feelings of inadequacy, questioning his worth and wondering if he had chosen the right path. Late nights at the office turned into gruelling battles against self-doubt. Every time he saw a peer get ahead without breaking a sweat, it stung—a constant reminder of a system that rewarded connections over capability.

His world took a disastrous turn when a series of thefts were reported within the company. Valuable equipment and machinery had gone missing, and the air was thick with whispers of betrayal echoing through the hallways. Aryan, already feeling the weight of being overlooked, became an easy target. A few of his colleagues, driven by their own agendas and perhaps a touch of jealousy at his dedication and work ethic, pointed fingers at him, weaving a narrative that painted him as the prime suspect.

The atmosphere in the office became hostile, and the once-familiar faces of his colleagues morphed into a chorus of suspicion. Management, caught in the whirlwind of rumours, acted swiftly and decisively. Aryan was called into a meeting, his heart racing with anxiety as he entered the room. Before he could even utter a word in his defence, the verdict was pronounced: he was unceremoniously kicked out of the airline.

The betrayal cut deep, not just because of the loss of his job—his hard-earned position—but because of the trust he had placed in the company and the very colleagues who had turned on him. The pain of being wrongfully accused felt like a crushing weight on his chest.

He walked out of the building for the last time, the world around him fading into a blur as he battled a storm of emotions—anger, disbelief, and profound sadness. It wasn't just a job he had lost; it was the hope he had harboured for a future built on hard work and integrity.

As he stood outside, the reality of his situation began to sink in. Aryan realized that this was not merely an end, but perhaps a twisted beginning. The betrayal ignited a fire within him, pushing him to reconsider his path. If the corporate world had turned its back on him, maybe it was time to forge his own destiny.

The shock of the unjust dismissal left Aryan reeling. He had poured his heart and soul into his work, believing that dedication and hard work would always pay off. Now, in the blink of an eye, everything had crumbled. The bitterness took root in his heart, transforming into a dark cloud that shadowed his thoughts and suffocated his spirit.

For the first time in his life, he felt a profound sense of despair. Nights turned into long, restless hours as he poured over job listings, sending out applications day and night. But the doors he once thought would be open to him were firmly shut. Each rejection email felt like a personal attack, a stark reminder of how quickly fortunes could change.

As days turned into weeks, and weeks into months, Aryan found himself spiralling into a state of hopelessness. It was as if his life was crumbling in front of his own eyes. The bright future he had envisioned—a life filled with achievement and recognition—was replaced by a haunting uncertainty. Friends who once reached out slowly faded away, unable to comprehend the depth of his struggle. The walls of his once-vibrant home now felt like a prison, echoing the silence of his despair.

With each passing day, Aryan's self-worth dwindled. He grappled with feelings of inadequacy and betrayal, haunted by the faces of those who had turned against him. The ambitions he had nurtured began to wither, and the fire in his belly dimmed to a flicker.

As Aryan's life continued to spiral downward, he found solace in the dimly lit corners of local bars. The intoxicating haze of alcohol temporarily numbed the pain of his failures, allowing him to escape the relentless weight of his circumstances. He frequented these establishments more often than he cared to admit, seeking refuge in the company of strangers and the bottom of a glass.

It was during one of these late-night escapades that he met Rajan, a man with a rough exterior and an air of danger that both intrigued and intimidated Aryan. Rajan was known in the underbelly of the city as the right-hand henchman of a notorious mafia don named Vikram. With a reputation that sent shivers down the spines of even the most hardened criminals, Vikram's influence loomed large over the city, casting a long shadow that enveloped everyone in its reach.

Initially, Aryan found himself drawn to Rajan's charisma, the way he carried himself with an unshakeable confidence. The tales Rajan spun were nothing short of mesmerizing, painting a vivid picture of a life filled with power and wealth, one that offered a stark contrast to the bleakness Aryan had been enduring.

He spoke of fast cars that roared like thunder, lavish parties that pulsated with life, and the kind of unbreakable loyalty that seemed like a brotherhood forged in fire.

"Imagine," Rajan said, his eyes gleaming with a feral light, "no more living pay-check to pay-check, no more begging for scraps. You'd have the city at your feet. You'd command respect, fear even. People would know your name."

The promise was intoxicating, far more appealing than the endless cycle of rejection and hopelessness that had become Aryan's daily existence. It was a siren call, pulling him deeper into a world where he could reclaim the power, he felt he had lost.

It is said that when a man is denied the life he believes in, he has no choice but to become an outlaw. Hence, every society gets the kind of criminal it deserves.

Depressed and naïve, Aryan agreed to meet his boss, the mafia don. It was a chilly evening when he stepped into the shadows, ready to face Vikram, the notorious figure whose name inspired both fear and respect across the criminal underbelly. The meeting took place in a dimly lit warehouse on the outskirts of town, an ominous setting that seemed to pulse with an unspoken tension. The air was thick with anticipation and the faint scent of betrayal lingered, casting a pall over the proceedings.

As Aryan entered, he was immediately struck by the sight of men gathered around a table strewn with maps, weapons, and a host of menacing paraphernalia that painted a vivid picture of the ruthless world he was about to step into. The flickering light from a single bulb illuminated the grim faces of men who had long forsaken any semblance of morality. A shiver ran down his spine as he realized that this was not the camaraderie he had envisioned; instead, it was a ruthless hierarchy where loyalty was often rewarded with violence.

Vikram sat at the head of the table, a man whose very presence commanded respect and fear. He was an imposing figure, his eyes cold and calculating, scanning Aryan with an intensity that made him feel both small and significant at the same time. As Aryan approached, he felt a mixture of excitement and dread churning within him. The allure of power beckoned, yet the reality of what lay before him was daunting.

"Welcome," Vikram said, his voice smooth yet edged with authority. "I've heard a lot about you, Aryan. You've had a rough ride, haven't you?" His gaze bore into Aryan, as if probing the depths of his soul. "But here, you can make a choice. You can either wallow in your misery or rise above it. We can give you the power you seek."

Aryan's heart raced as he considered Vikram's words. This was the moment he had been waiting for—the chance to reclaim his life, to carve out a new identity. Yet, beneath the surface of Vikram's promises lay a hidden darkness, an unsettling reminder of the moral abyss he was about to plunge into.

"Join us," Vikram continued, leaning back in his chair, exuding an air of control. "Prove your loyalty, and you'll have everything you've ever wanted—wealth, power, respect. But betray us, and you'll find out just how ruthless we can be."

As Aryan stood there, the weight of the decision pressed heavily on him. The thrill of what could be danced tantalizingly close, but so did the grim reality of the life he was about to enter.

Aryan's heart raced as he absorbed Vikram's words. The promise of action, of finally being seen as more than just a victim of circumstance, ignited a spark within him. Yet, beneath that spark lay an unsettling sense of foreboding. "I'm ready," he replied, the words escaping his lips with a mix of eagerness and trepidation.

Vikram's eyes narrowed, scrutinizing Aryan as if trying to gauge the truth behind his bravado. He leaned in, his gaze unyielding. “You'll need to prove yourself. We need sharp shooters for our gang—a job that require precision and discretion. And a lot of guts. Are you ready to make your mark?”

Aryan's heart raced at Vikram's words. The promise of power and acceptance hung tantalizingly in the air, but a nagging voice in the back of his mind cautioned him about the depths of this new world. "I'm ready," he repeated, trying to mask his unease with bravado.

Vikram's lips curled into a predatory smile. "Good. We're targeting a rival gang tonight—send a message that we won't be trifled with. Are you prepared for what those entails?"

As Aryan nodded, a mix of excitement and dread surged through him. The prospect of action thrilled him, but the gravity of the task weighed heavily on his conscience. He had been searching for purpose, yet this was a path strewn with danger and moral ambiguity.

The plan was laid out with precision. Vikram detailed their approach, the timings, the weapons they would use, and how to secure the area. Aryan listened intently, absorbing every word, trying to envision the steps ahead. He could feel the adrenaline pooling in his veins, igniting a primal instinct within him.

"Remember, this is not just a job; it's a test of loyalty," Vikram warned, locking eyes with each member of the crew. "If you succeed, you'll earn your place among us. Fail, and you'll be on the receiving end of our wrath."

As they prepped for the operation, Aryan felt the tension in the air thickening. He was no longer just a man seeking revenge; he was on the brink of becoming someone feared and respected. Yet, as the team gathered their weapons and strategized, a flicker of doubt gnawed at him. This was a violent world, and he was stepping into the heart of it.

The night was dark, the streets eerily quiet as they drove toward the rival gang's hideout. Aryan sat in the backseat, his mind racing. Images of his old life flashed before him—his family, his dreams, the man he used to be. He had fought hard for everything, but now, was he willing to sacrifice it all for this?

As they arrived, Vikram motioned for silence. The team slipped from the vehicle, moving like shadows in the night. Aryan's pulse quickened as they approached the rundown warehouse, its silhouette looming ominously against the moonlit sky.

Vikram led the charge, his presence commanding and fierce. Aryan followed closely, his heart pounding in rhythm with the footsteps around him. They crept toward the entrance, and Aryan could hear muffled voices inside—their target was just within reach.

With a swift gesture, Vikram signalled for them to move in. The moment was upon them, and Aryan felt a surge of adrenaline. As they burst through the doors, chaos erupted. Gunshots rang out, the air thick with the acrid smell of gunpowder. Aryan's instincts kicked in as he ducked and dodged, adrenaline fuelling his every move.

In the frenzy, he caught sight of a figure across the room—a rival gang member. Everything slowed down, and in that split second, Aryan drew his weapon, feeling the weight of the moment. He could hear Vikram's voice in the back of his mind, urging him to act. The line between survival and morality blurred, and he squeezed the trigger.

The shot rang out, echoing in the warehouse, and time resumed. The figure collapsed, and Aryan stood frozen, the reality of what he had just done crashing over him. The thrill of the moment began to fade, replaced by a profound sense of dread. He had crossed a line that couldn't be uncrossed.

The chaos continued around him, men shouting and fighting, but Aryan felt detached, as if watching from a distance. He had sought power and respect, but at what cost?

As the operation concluded and the team emerged victorious, Aryan's thoughts spiralled into a storm of guilt and regret. He had proven himself to Vikram, but in doing so, he had lost a piece of himself. The darkness of this new life beckoned, and he was left standing at the edge, wondering if he could ever find his way back to the light.

Aryan ended up being a sharp-shooter in the underworld. He started accepting *'Supari's'*, which was the street term for killing people for money. Aryan made a lot of friends in the underworld and, for a time, he felt a sense of belonging he hadn't experienced in years. The thrill of living on the edge, coupled with the camaraderie of his newfound companions, created an intoxicating atmosphere. Nights were filled with laughter, stories of past exploits, and the intoxicating aroma of smoke-filled rooms. It was a stark contrast to the loneliness that had plagued him after losing his job in the aviation industry.

The gun became Aryan's closest companion, a cold piece of metal that somehow warmed him with a newfound sense of power. Every time he held it, he felt a surge of confidence, a promise of respect that had eluded him in the corporate world. The weight of the weapon in his hand transformed from a mere object into an extension of his own will—a tool for asserting dominance in a world where might often overshadowed right.

He immersed himself in training, dedicating countless hours to honing his skills. Under Rajan's watchful eye, Aryan practiced relentlessly, mastering a range of firearms—from handguns to rifles. Each day at the makeshift shooting range, he pushed himself further, driven by a blend of ambition and the intoxicating adrenaline of the lifestyle he had chosen. With every bullseye, he shed pieces of his former self, transforming into a sharpshooter whose name soon echoed through the underworld.

As whispers of Aryan's prowess spread, he earned a reputation that demanded attention. The gang's leadership took note; he was no longer just another recruit but a valuable asset. Respect was hard to come by in the criminal hierarchy, yet Aryan's talent carved out a place for him, granting him a status that many sought but few attained.

Mercilessness became his biggest asset and sympathy his greatest adversity. And boy, was he good at it. Aryan rose through the ranks of crime, climbing the ladder at a nifty speed, his skills as a sharp-shooter earning him respect and notoriety. He quickly became known for his unwavering loyalty and his knack for handling high-stakes jobs with precision. In the gritty underbelly of the city, where chaos reigned, he thrived in the darkness, feeling alive for the first time in years. His loyalty to Vikram solidified his position in the gang, and he quickly became one of the don's most trusted enforcers. Together, they executed a series of high-stakes jobs, each one more dangerous than the last.

The world he inhabited was a stark contrast to the one he had known growing up—a realm where survival hinged on brutality and intimidation. Each day was a gamble, a game of cat and mouse where trust was scarce, and the stakes were life and death. He learned quickly that there were only two cardinal rules: never deny the boss and never rat out your syndicate to the police. Breaking either would lead to swift and unforgiving consequences.

Aryan bravely carried out risky contract killings at the behest of his boss, quickly cementing his reputation in the underworld. His rapid rise not only gained him a significant amount of street cred but also turned him into a figure of intrigue. On the one hand, some people looked at him with awe and admiration; on the other, there were equal measures of envy and disdain. Aryan was now a dual figure in the eyes of the world—an admired enforcer and a feared assassin.

As "Aryan Bhai," he became a name that echoed in the alleys and backrooms of the city, whispered in both reverence and fear. Those who feared him often spoke of his uncanny precision, his cold demeanour, and his unwavering loyalty to Vikram, the mafia don. To his acquaintances, he was a man who had seen the depths of despair and had clawed his way to the top, but to his enemies, he was a ruthless predator who showed no mercy.

With each successful job, Aryan earned not just money but also a sort of twisted fame. The financial rewards were substantial; he bought luxurious cars, expensive clothes, and made it a point to flaunt his wealth. He partied in the most exclusive clubs, and his name became synonymous with power. Yet, beneath the surface of this newfound life, Aryan grappled with an increasing sense of discontent. The glamour of being "Aryan Bhai" felt hollow at times, overshadowed by the grim realities of the choices he had made.

He surrounded himself with a circle of loyal allies, each one a reflection of the life he now led. They were a motley crew of fellow criminals, each with their own stories of how they had ended up in this world. They celebrated his successes, raising glasses in his honour, but Aryan couldn't shake the nagging feeling that this lifestyle was unsustainable. Trust was a scarce commodity, and betrayal loomed around every corner.

The power dynamics of the underworld were volatile. New players emerged, eager to stake their claim, and rival gangs constantly plotted against one another. With Aryan's rising fame came increasing scrutiny. Other gangs viewed him as a threat, and some even plotted to take him down. This atmosphere of danger became a part of his daily life, heightening his senses but also amplifying his paranoia. Every shadow felt like a potential enemy, every whisper a warning.

Despite the fame and fortune, Aryan's nights were often haunted by the ghosts of his past. The faces of those he had taken down flashed before his eyes—each one a reminder of his moral decline. Late at night, he would sit alone, the weight of his decisions pressing heavily on his chest. He could hear echoes of laughter from his childhood, memories of running through the streets with Chetan, dreaming of a future full of promise. How had it all come to this?

Aryan's days blurred into a haze of meetings at dimly lit bars and backroom deals, each encounter more dangerous than the last. In this world, loyalty was a fickle concept, and trust was a currency he could no longer afford. He navigated through the smoky rooms filled with shadows, surrounded by men who were equally hungry for power and respect. Each handshake and nod was steeped in unspoken agreements, a delicate dance of mutual benefit in a place where betrayal lurked in every corner.

His lifestyle became a whirlwind of excess. He feasted on the spoils of his newfound status. Alcohol flowed freely, and women flocked to him, drawn by his reputation as "Aryan Bhai." They were eager to bask in the glow of his notoriety, providing fleeting companionship in the chaotic life he had chosen.

But soon, the allure of this lifestyle spiralled into something darker. Introduced to drugs by the unsavoury characters he surrounded himself with, Aryan found solace in substances that dulled the edges of reality. The high offered a temporary escape from the weight of his choices and the ghosts that haunted him. It became a part of his daily ritual—an essential element in the cycle of eat, drink, kill, party, and repeat. Each day, he convinced himself that he was invincible, that he had found the freedom he had long sought.

In this altered state, Aryan felt triumphant. The promise made to him when he joined the underworld echoed in his mind: all his problems would vanish. In many ways, it seemed true. He was no longer the downtrodden man seeking employment; he was a force to be reckoned with, a name spoken in hushed tones.

But only the naïve believe that crime triumphs, right?

One fine evening, as Aryan returned to his apartment, the heavy thud of boots echoed behind him. Before he could react, officers descended upon him, handcuffing him and dragging him into the harsh reality of a police cruiser. The clang of the heavy cell door echoed in Aryan's ears as he was thrown into the grim confines of the police station. The moment he stepped inside, he felt the weight of despair press down on him like an iron shroud. The atmosphere was thick with tension, a palpable reminder of the law's unforgiving nature. Aryan had played the game of shadows for too long, and now, he was paying the price.

As the guards walked away, leaving him alone with his thoughts, the reality of his situation began to sink in. He was surrounded by hardened criminals, men who wore their experiences like badges, and the air was heavy with the scent of sweat and desperation. Aryan's heart raced; he was acutely aware that he was now at the mercy of the very system he had evaded for so long.

Inside the jail, Aryan learned of the full extent of the charges against him. They included murder, stemming from the shooting that had taken place during a chaotic gang war. An innocent bystander had been caught in the crossfire, and the weight of the accusation felt like a vice tightening around his chest. This time, he was innocent—an unfortunate victim of circumstance, dragged into a narrative that twisted the truth beyond recognition.

Hours bled into days, each moment stretching out like an eternity as the relentless police interrogation continued. Aryan was subjected to a barrage of accusations, their voices a cacophony of hostility that echoed off the cold, unforgiving walls. They prowled around him like wolves, baring their teeth with threats that hung heavy in the air, attempting to peel away his resolve.

But Aryan stood firm, his heart pounding in his chest like a war drum. The brutality of their tactics only fuelled his determination to remain silent. Each insult, each scream aimed at breaking his spirit, was met with a steely gaze that refused to falter. He knew what was at stake—betraying his syndicate, his boss Vikram, would unleash a torrent of consequences that could obliterate not just him but everyone he held dear.

The pain he endured—both physical and mental—was excruciating, yet it was dwarfed by the shadow of fear that loomed larger in his mind. The thought of retribution, of the wrath that would befall him and his loved ones, kept his lips sealed. He steeled himself against the brutal onslaught, every accusation a reminder of the dark world he inhabited, where loyalty was currency and silence was a lifeline.

Each night, as he lay on the cold concrete floor, Aryan reflected on the choices that had led him to this dark place. Memories of his childhood flooded back—the carefree days we spent together, the laughter, and dreams that now felt like distant echoes. A part of him longed to escape this life, to find a way back to the person he once was. But how? The walls of his prison felt insurmountable, both literally and metaphorically.

In the oppressive confines of the jail, Aryan felt the walls closing in on him. The days stretched into an unending blur; each moment filled with the harshness of prison life. Conversations were scarce, and the only sounds were the distant clanging of metal doors and the low murmurs of fellow inmates, each lost in their own struggles. It was becoming increasingly difficult for Aryan to keep hoping for the light at the end of the tunnel.

But within this grim reality, Aryan had heard whispers of a hidden underworld—one where drugs and alcohol could provide a fleeting escape from this bitter reality. At first, he dismissed the rumours, knowing the risks involved in consuming alcohol in jail. It could be disastrous for him if he was caught, giving the jail authorities even more compelling reasons to torture him. Although he had indulged in such activities earlier, he tried to abstain for now.

One evening, while sitting in the common area, Aryan noticed a small group gathered in a corner, their voices low and conspiratorial. He strained to catch snippets of their conversation, words like "moonshine" and "stash" floating through the air. It piqued his interest, and soon enough, he found himself drawn into their orbit.

A man named Benny, known for his connections, approached Aryan. "You look like you could use a drink," he said, a knowing grin spreading across his face. "I can get you something special—just a little something to take the edge off."

Aryan hesitated, a mixture of excitement and apprehension coursing through him. But the idea of momentarily escaping the relentless reality of prison was too tempting to resist. He nodded, and Benny led him to a dimly lit corner of the yard, away from the watchful eyes of the guards.

Benny produced a small vial filled with a clear liquid. “Moonshine,” he declared, handing it over. “Trust me, it’s the good stuff.”

With a deep breath, Aryan took the vial and raised it to his lips. The liquid burned as it slid down his throat, a fierce heat spreading through him. For a moment, everything else faded away—the stress, the uncertainty, the memories of his past. He felt a wave of warmth and a sense of camaraderie with the other inmates, as if they were all in this together.

As the nights passed, Aryan found himself drawn deeper into this world. started spending his savings on alcohol, revelling in the brief moments of euphoria they provided.

One night, after consuming more moonshine than he could handle, Aryan stumbled into the common area, feeling invincible. The laughter and noise buzzed around him, and he found himself the centre of attention. He began to boast about his past, sharing tales of his life before prison—his adventures of being the dreaded ‘Aryan Bhai’.

But the intoxication blurred his judgment. As he became louder, he caught the eye of Rakesh, a notorious inmate known for his volatility. Rakesh approached, a scowl on his face. "You think you can just waltz in here and take over?" he challenged, his tone threatening.

"Just having a little fun," Aryan replied, slurring his words but trying to maintain an air of bravado. "You got a problem with that?"

The inmates who had gathered around them anticipating a good fight, started cheering loudly. Cries of "Fight! Fight!" started echoing in the area. Hearing the commotion, the guards rushed in and forced the inmates into retreat. The crowd was disappointed, as a violent fight breaking out within the confines of jail was the best kind of entertainment which they could have wished for. They weren't aware that their wish would come true the very next day.

Next afternoon, Aryan was sitting on the worn concrete bench in the common area, his thoughts racing. He had been trying to keep his head down, avoid conflicts, and navigate the dangerous dynamics of prison life. But thanks to his drunk antics, the atmosphere was tense. The air was thick with whispers of gang rivalries and shifting alliances.

That day, a group of men gathered near the entrance, their laughter echoing ominously. Among them was Rakesh, a notorious inmate with a reputation for violence. Aryan had heard stories about him—how he ruled the yard with an iron fist, and how anyone who crossed him faced dire consequences. Last night, he narrowly avoided getting into an ugly fight with him. The end result wouldn't have been good, he realised.

As Aryan tried to focus on a book, he felt a presence looming over him. He looked up to see Rakesh staring down at him, a smug smile on his face. "What are you reading, Aryan Bhai?" he taunted, his voice dripping with mockery.

"It's none of your business," Aryan replied, keeping his tone steady despite the knot tightening in his stomach.

Rakesh leaned closer, his menacing grin widening. "You think you're better than us just because you are a don's pet?"

Aryan felt a surge of anger. "Just leave me alone, or else you'll be really sorry."

That seemed to amuse Rakesh. He laughed, a harsh, cruel sound that echoed in the quiet yard. "Brave words for someone who's about to get hurt."

In an instant, Rakesh signalled to his crew, and they surrounded Aryan, cutting off any escape route. Aryan's heart raced as he stood up, preparing to defend himself. He knew he had to fight back or risk being a victim.

"Come on, let's see what you've got, sharp shooter," Rakesh sneered, stepping forward with a menacing glare.

Without warning, Rakesh lunged at him, fists swinging. Aryan barely had time to react as he dodged the first punch, feeling the rush of air as it whooshed past his face. Instinct kicked in; he fought back, landing a solid punch to Rakesh's jaw. The other inmates gasped, surprised by Aryan's quick retaliation.

But Rakesh was unfazed. He recovered quickly, anger flashing in his eyes. "You've got some fight in you, huh? Let's see how long you can last."

As they exchanged blows, Aryan's adrenaline surged. He was aware of the crowd forming around them, their shouts and cheers fuelling the chaos. Rakesh was stronger, but Aryan was determined. He ducked another punch and countered with a swift kick to Rakesh's knee, sending him stumbling backward.

But Rakesh was relentless. He charged at Aryan again, and this time, Aryan felt the impact as Vikram tackled him to the ground. They rolled on the concrete, grappling for control. Aryan struggled to push Rakesh off him, panic rising as he realized the gravity of the situation. He had to survive this.

Suddenly, Aryan caught a glimpse of something glinting on the ground—an improvised weapon, a shard of metal from a broken pipe. It was a dangerous temptation, but he knew he had to act fast. With a surge of determination, he managed to get his hands on it, but in doing so, he exposed himself to a more vicious assault.

Rakesh's crew closed in, their shouts becoming a cacophony of violence. Aryan felt his heart pounding in his chest, knowing he had only seconds to make a choice. He couldn't let himself be overpowered. With a primal instinct, he thrust the makeshift weapon toward Rakesh, narrowly avoiding a potentially fatal blow.

The shard scraped against Rakesh's arm, causing him to recoil in shock. In that split second, Aryan pushed himself up, adrenaline coursing through his veins. He fought his way to his feet, ready to face whatever came next.

Rakesh, now furious and wounded, charged again, his eyes wild with rage. "You think you can get away with this?"

With the crowd roaring around them, Aryan braced himself. He swung the metal shard again, but this time, he aimed for Rakesh's leg, desperate to immobilize him. The weapon connected, and Rakesh staggered, his expression shifting from anger to disbelief.

Taking advantage of Rakesh's momentary weakness, Aryan lunged forward, tackling him to the ground. The two rolled in a frenzy, fists flying, as the surrounding inmates cheered wildly. Aryan felt a surge of power, knowing that this was not just a fight for survival, but a fight for his dignity.

In a final burst of strength, Aryan pinned Rakesh down, the shard glinting dangerously close to the man's throat. "This ends now," Aryan said, his voice steady despite the chaos around him.

Rakesh's eyes widened in realization. The crowd fell silent, the tension palpable. Aryan felt a rush of victory, knowing he had turned the tide. He released Rakesh, pushing himself away as he stood up, breathing heavily.

As the guards finally arrived, the chaos dissipated. Aryan had won not just the fight but also strengthened the fear and respect among the inmates. It was unlikely that he would be attacked again, at least for a while.

However, his worries were not showing any signs of coming to an end. Days stretched into an agonizing blur, each moment weighed down by uncertainty and fear. Aryan found himself trapped in a world that felt increasingly claustrophobic, the walls of his cell closing in around him. The stale air was thick with despair, but a flicker of hope ignited within him when he received a message from Vikram's men.

Through a guarded whisper, the words reached him: "Vikram is looking for ways to get you out on bail." Relief washed over him momentarily, a balm against the gnawing anxiety that had taken root in his heart. But as days passed and the echoes of that promise faded into silence, the hope turned to dread.

Weeks slipped by without further word. The absence of communication felt like a betrayal, a sign that perhaps the loyalty he had offered so freely was not reciprocated. Aryan's mind raced with fear—was Vikram truly searching for a way out for him, or had he been lying.

After what felt like an eternity, Aryan was granted a brief respite—a visit from a lawyer, Mrs. Malhotra.

Mrs. Malhotra sat at her desk, the dim light of her office casting sharp shadows across the stacks of case files. She was an astute lawyer, renowned for her ability to navigate the murky waters of criminal defence. With a reputation built on a series of high-profile victories, she had successfully defended some of the most notorious gangsters in the city. Her clients revered her, while her opponents often regarded her with a mix of respect and disdain. She was a force to be reckoned with—pragmatic, strategic, and utterly fearless.

Today, however, her attention was focused on a case that was different from her usual fare. Aryan's situation was precarious, and the stakes were high. He was a rising figure in the underworld, a man whose loyalty and silence were invaluable commodities. Yet, there was a looming threat: Aryan's potential betrayal could unravel a carefully constructed empire. Vikram, her long-time client and the mafia don who had brought Aryan into the fold, had made it clear that Aryan needed to be protected at all costs.

"Mrs. Malhotra," Vikram had said, his voice steady and commanding, "this boy cannot be allowed to speak against us. You must ensure he remains quiet, no matter what. Do what you do best."

The pressure weighed heavily on her shoulders. While she had taken on difficult cases before, this one felt particularly charged. The lives of many hung in the balance—not just Aryan's, but also those of her family and her own career. A misstep could lead to disastrous repercussions, both legally and personally. She knew very well that she couldn't afford to get in the bad books of the underworld. Vikram was known to set an example out of the people who betrayed him, or let him down. There were many instances when their families had to pay the price for their mistakes. Mrs. Malhotra had just one person in the world whom she could call as family, her beloved daughter Vani. She couldn't risk doing anything which would endanger Vani, not even a strand of her hair.

Aryan, on the other hand, was desperate and vulnerable. After being jailed, he was navigating a world that had turned upside down. The underworld that had once seemed alluring was now filled with threats and shadows. He needed someone in his corner, someone who could understand the nuances of his precarious position. When he first met Mrs. Malhotra, he was struck by her confidence and composure. She was no-nonsense, with a sharp gaze that seemed to see right through him.

"Mr. Aryan," she began during their first meeting, her tone crisp, "you are in a very difficult position. You need to cooperate with me if you want to navigate this situation successfully."

Aryan nodded, the weight of her words sinking in. He could feel the gravity of the situation pressing down on him. “I understand,” he replied, trying to project a sense of confidence he didn’t fully feel. “I just want to make sure I don’t end up in jail for a long time.”

“Your silence is paramount. The police want names, and I assure you, they won’t hesitate to use intimidation tactics. You must not give in.” She leaned in slightly, her expression unwavering. “Trust me, I have dealt with worse.”

As they prepared for the upcoming trial, Aryan couldn’t help but notice the web of connections that surrounded Mrs. Malhotra. She moved with a confidence that suggested she was well-versed in the intricacies of the criminal underworld. There were whispers of her previous cases, stories of how she had maneuverer through threats and pressures to protect her clients.

Aryan felt at ease now. Fortune finally seemed to be favouring him.

However, things changed very, very quickly. Fortune is a fickle mistress. Just when things seem to be going well, she abandons us. Just when things seem like they can't get any worse, she piles on; and then, sometimes, we're caught completely by surprise when a seemingly impossible situation turns around.

Within a few weeks the courtroom trials had begun. Aryan was warned by his lawyer that it would take many such trials, to even hope for a chance to secure his bail. He understood that he needed to be patient, and Mrs. Malhotra would take care of the rest. What he didn't know however, was that everything was going to change very soon.

The courtroom buzzed with tension as the trial unfolded. Mrs. Malhotra stood tall, her reputation as a formidable lawyer on the line, but the growing pressure from the media and public scrutiny began to take its toll. As the trial progressed, the headlines became more sensational, focusing not only on Aryan's past but also on Mrs. Malhotra's connections to the underworld. Whispers of corruption and conflict of interest filled the air, and soon enough, the bar association began to take notice.

"Mrs. Malhotra," her assistant called during a brief recess, urgency lacing his voice. "You need to see this." He handed her a newspaper, the headline blaring accusations against her, painting her as a criminal's accomplice.

Her heart sank as she read the words. It wasn't just sensationalism; the bar was considering an investigation into her practices. The threats of suspension hung like a dark cloud over her, casting shadows on her illustrious career.

The next day, as the trial resumed, the pressure became unbearable. The prosecutor, sensing her vulnerability, launched a blistering attack, attempting to undermine her credibility. "Your Honor, it seems we have a lawyer here who is more concerned with protecting her clients and earning her money, rather than upholding the law," he said, turning the courtroom's gaze toward her.

Mrs. Malhotra remained composed, but she could feel the weight of scrutiny pressing down on her. Every move she made was now under a microscope, and the courtroom had become a battleground not just for Aryan's freedom but for her career as well as her reputation. She had more at stake than she was willing to.

As the trial continued, the media frenzy escalated. Reporters camped outside the courthouse, eager to capture every moment, every detail, and to magnify the slightest misstep. Mrs. Malhotra's phone rang incessantly with calls from the bar association, demanding explanations and assurances.

One afternoon, she received an urgent summons to meet with the bar's disciplinary committee. That was the precise moment when she snapped and made the decision. The air in her office felt heavy with dread as she realized she could no longer represent Aryan without risking everything she had worked for. She was going to withdraw from this case.

Things were spiralling downwards for Aryan at a rapid pace. Just when he thought the situation couldn't get any worse, he received the news that Mrs. Malhotra had withdrawn herself from his case. Panic set in as he realized that no other decent lawyer was willing to take it on. Some were deterred by the potential bad publicity that could tarnish their reputations, while others feared the repercussions from Vikram, who had a notorious reputation of not sparing people who messed up.

Once again, his luck had deserted him. He had heard rumours that the jury was going to convict him without a fair trial, and he faced the possibility of being hanged, or worse, spend the rest of his life in jail.

CHAPTER 5
ARYAN - VANI

The office was dimly lit, the late afternoon sun casting long shadows across the room as Mrs. Malhotra sat alone at her desk, her fingers trembling over the keyboard. The pressure had become unbearable. Whispers filled the corridors of the bar council, and the media had descended upon her like vultures, eager to feast on the scandal surrounding Aryan's case. She had been drawn into a web of crime and deceit, and now, with a heavy heart, she knew she had to make a choice.

With a deep breath, she clicked "send" on her resignation letter, a sense of finality washing over her. The weight of betrayal pressed down on her like a suffocating fog. She had built her career on integrity, yet here she was, abandoning her client to save her own reputation. As she stared at the screen, the reality of her decision sank in, and she felt a pang of guilt. But she had to protect herself.

Unbeknownst to her, a storm was brewing just beyond her office walls. Vikram, the don whose world revolved around power and fear, had been watching her every move. Betrayal was a currency he could not afford, and he was not one to take such a slight lightly. The moment he learned of her resignation, his rage ignited like wildfire. He made a swift decision—she would pay for her disloyalty.

That evening, as darkness enveloped the city, Mrs. Malhotra gathered her things, her heart still heavy with the weight of her choice. Outside, the streets hummed with life, but an unsettling sense of foreboding hung in the air. She stepped into her car, the engine humming to life, unaware that she was being watched.

A few blocks away, Vikram's men lay in wait, their eyes trained on her every movement. They communicated silently, their expressions grim and determined. As she drove down the quiet street, the tension was palpable; a predator stalking its prey.

Suddenly, the world exploded in a cacophony of sound. A shot rang out, sharp and echoing, slicing through the evening air. The bullet shattered the passenger window, the glass exploding in a shower of glittering shards. Time slowed as Mrs. Malhotra instinctively ducked, her heart racing with primal fear.

The bullet struck her shoulder, searing pain radiating through her body. A gasp escaped her lips as she felt the warmth of blood seeping through her clothes, each heartbeat amplifying the agony. She slammed on the brakes, the car skidding to a halt as the reality of the situation engulfed her.

"Vikram!" she managed to whisper, the name a haunting echo in her mind. The betrayal felt like a noose tightening around her neck. How had she gotten to this point? In her quest to protect herself, she had invited danger into her life.

Panic surged through her as she fumbled for her phone, her hands shaking uncontrollably. The weight of her decision loomed large as she dialled for help, her vision beginning to blur at the edges. Sirens wailed in the distance, growing louder, but in that moment, all she could focus on was the sharp, gnawing pain that consumed her.

She thought of her daughter, Vani, and a wave of regret washed over her. "I'm so sorry, Vani," she gasped, feeling the darkness creep in. The sirens were closer now, but they felt distant, like a fading dream. The world around her was spinning, and she fought to stay conscious, to hold on to the last threads of her reality.

As the ambulance arrived, paramedics rushed to her side, their voices muffled and distant. They worked quickly, but the fear that gripped her heart was unyielding. Would she see her daughter again? Would she have a chance to make things right?

In the ambulance, the bright lights flashed above her like a strobe, casting eerie shadows across the cramped space. The sirens wailed, a relentless noise that echoed the chaos of her thoughts. Mrs. Malhotra felt the cool metal of the gurney beneath her, the jarring motion making the pain in her shoulder flare with every bump.

Images of her daughter, Vani, filled her mind, each memory a bittersweet reminder of the love and connection they shared. Vani's laughter, her bright eyes full of ambition, and the late-night talks that stretched into dawn—all of it was at risk now. A deep, gnawing fear took root in her heart. What would happen to Vani if she didn't survive this? Who would protect her from the dark world that had ensnared them both?

"Please, God," she whispered, her voice barely audible over the sirens. "Protect my daughter. Keep her safe." The prayer felt like a fragile thread, a last plea for mercy in the face of overwhelming despair.

As the paramedics worked feverishly, shouting orders and asking her questions, Mrs. Malhotra felt a wave of dizziness wash over her. The pain was a distant roar, overshadowed by a creeping darkness that began to pull her under. She struggled to hold onto consciousness, to fight through the encroaching void, but it was a losing battle.

Her eyelids grew heavy, and despite her best efforts, she felt herself slipping away. Vani's face flickered in her mind, a beacon of light in the storm, but it dimmed as the darkness closed in. "I love you, Vani," she murmured, the words barely escaping her lips as her vision blurred, fading into a sea of black.

The sterile scent of antiseptic filled the air as Vani rushed into the hospital, her heart pounding in her chest. Tears streamed down her face, blurring her vision as she made her way through the stark corridors. The police had called just hours before, their words like ice slicing through her heart: "Your mother's been shot. You need to come to the hospital immediately."

Every step felt like a mile as she navigated the cold, clinical space, her mind racing with fear and disbelief. How had it come to this? Why hadn't she been able to protect her mother?

When she finally reached her mother's room, Vani pushed the door open to find her mom lying on the hospital bed, pale and still. A wave of nausea washed over her as she took in the sight—IV drips, monitors beeping, the stark reality of her mother's vulnerability.

"Mom!" she cried, her voice breaking as she rushed to her side. Vani's knees buckled, and she fell to the floor beside the bed, overwhelmed by shock and despair. She felt a crushing weight in her chest as she clutched her mother's hand, praying for warmth to return to her skin. "Please, please wake up. I need you."

Vani had always loved her mother fiercely, even when their views clashed. She had warned Mrs. Malhotra time and again about the dangers of representing clients like Vikram and the mafia. The allure of money and fame had clouded her judgment, but Vani had known the risks. She had watched her mother dance dangerously close to the flames, but this—this was a nightmare she had never imagined.

"I should have done more," she sobbed, the weight of guilt crashing down on her. "I should have been there for you."

The nurse entered; her expression serious but compassionate. "Miss Malhotra, the doctors are taking your mother into surgery. It's a serious operation, but we're doing everything we can."

Vani nodded numbly, her heart racing as she tried to gather her thoughts. She needed to be strong, for her mother's sake. She wiped her tears and whispered a silent prayer, her hands clasped together as if the act could somehow summon the strength her mother needed. "God, please save her. If you do, I promise I'll do anything to keep her safe from now on."

Time stretched painfully as she waited outside the operation theatre, pacing the floor, each tick of the clock echoing like a drum in her ears. She envisioned her mother, vibrant and strong, fighting against the darkness that threatened to engulf her. Vani remembered all the moments they had shared—laughter, tears, and the unbreakable bond of love. She couldn't lose her. Not now.

Four agonizing hours passed before a surgeon finally emerged, his expression a mix of exhaustion and relief. Vani's heart leaped into her throat as she approached him, desperate for news.

"Your mother is out of danger," he said, the words hitting her like a lifeline. "The bullet had pierced her shoulder joint and lodged near her neck, but we managed to remove it. She'll need a few weeks in the hospital for recovery, but she's a fighter. You can see her soon."

Tears of relief streamed down Vani's face as she let out a shaky breath. "Thank you," she whispered, her heart swelling with gratitude. The fear that had consumed her began to ebb, replaced by a flicker of hope.

As she was led into her mother's room, Vani felt a rush of emotion. Mrs. Malhotra lay pale but stable, her chest rising and falling in a gentle rhythm. Vani approached the bed, clutching her mother's hand tightly. "I'm here, Mom," she said, her voice choked with emotion. "I love you. We'll get through this together."

In that moment, Vani vowed to herself that things would change. She would protect her mother from the dangers of her past choices.

With her heart still racing, she leaned in closer, whispering a promise to the woman who had always been her guiding star. "I'll make sure you're safe, I promise. You're going to be okay."

As her mother remained in a fragile slumber, Vani felt the resolve solidify within her. The battle was far from over, but she was ready to fight, not just for her mother, but for their future together.

The fluorescent lights flickered overhead as Vani paced the hospital corridor, her heart racing from the conversation with Vikram. She could still feel the chill in his voice, like ice running through her veins. The news of her mother's survival had brought her a flicker of hope, but that hope was quickly extinguished by the shadows of threats looming over her.

"Vani," Vikram's voice cut through her thoughts like a blade when she answered the call. "I see your mother has survived. But let's be clear: she won't be around much longer if you don't do as I say."

"Stop it!" she shouted, her voice breaking. "Leave her out of this, Vikram! She's been through enough already!"

His laughter was cold and calculated. "You misunderstand, my dear. Your mother is a liability now. She knows too much, and I can't afford to let her live if you refuse to cooperate. You have a choice to make."

Vani's heart sank. The realization that her mother's life was now a bargaining chip in a deadly game filled her with dread. "What do you want from me?" she asked, trying to keep her voice steady.

"I need you to represent Aryan in court," Vikram said matter-of-factly. "Get him out of prison at all costs. He's my most valuable asset, and you will ensure his freedom. If you do this for me, I'll keep your mother safe."

The world spun around her. Vani had heard stories about Aryan, the notorious criminal linked to the very underbelly of the city her mother had once tried to represent. He was a man of shadows, and the thought of defending him made her stomach churn.

"Please, Vikram, don't do this," she pleaded. "There must be another way. I'll do anything else, just don't hurt her!"

"You know how this works, Vani," he replied, his tone unyielding. "This is the only way. You get Aryan out, or you'll lose your mother. Simple as that."

Tears brimmed in her eyes as desperation clawed at her heart. She couldn't lose her mother—not after everything they had been through. "I'll do it," she said, the words escaping her lips like a quiet surrender. "I'll represent Aryan in court. Just promise me you'll keep my mom safe."

"Excellent choice," Vikram said, a satisfied smirk evident in his voice. "I'll be in touch with the details. Remember, Vani—your mother's life depends on your success."

As he hung up, Vani felt a hollow ache in her chest. She leaned against the wall, her breath coming in short gasps. The weight of her decision bore down on her like a heavy shroud. To protect her mother, she had to plunge headfirst into the world of crime, representing a man who was the very embodiment of danger.

In the quiet of the corridor, she wiped her tears and took a deep breath. This was a fight for her mother's life, and she needed to prepare. Vani wouldn't just represent Aryan; she would uncover the truth behind his case, navigate the treacherous waters of the legal system, and confront the dark undercurrents that had ensnared their lives. She decided to start preparing for the case ahead. But first, she had to go and meet Aryan.

Before meeting Aryan, Vani had built up a strong mental image of him based on what she had heard. To her, he was just another hardened criminal—ruthless, self-serving, and entirely lacking in compassion. She envisioned a man who would think nothing of tossing money at a lawyer to buy his freedom, indifferent to the impact of his actions on others. The very thought of defending someone like him repulsed her; she believed that individuals like Aryan deserved to be locked away, far from civilized society, where they couldn't inflict harm.

But life had thrust her into a corner. Vikram's chilling warning hung over her like a dark cloud: her life and her mother's life were at stake if she failed to secure Aryan's freedom. With no choice but to step into the world of criminal law, Vani buried her personal convictions and set to work.

She immersed herself in the case files, poring over the evidence and details with an intensity born of desperation. Each paper was a window into Aryan's crimes, a world that she had only seen through the lens of her biases. She felt the weight of responsibility settle heavily on her shoulders, forcing her to confront the stark reality of her situation.

After long hours of sifting through documents, Vani prepared the necessary paperwork for the court representation. The urgency of the case fuelled her determination. But as she finished, a flicker of doubt crept in. What if she was wrong about Aryan? What if there was more to his story than she could see?

The next day, she steeled herself for the meeting.

Vani stood in front of the imposing structure of the prison, her heart racing as she prepared to enter. The steel-grey walls loomed over her, a stark reminder of the world she was about to step into—a world fraught with danger and deception. Yet, beneath her apprehension lay a determination that burned bright. She was not just stepping into a prison; she was stepping into a pivotal moment of her life, one that could alter the course of both her future and her mother's.

At just twenty-four, Vani had made a name for herself as a lawyer, earning respect for her sharp intellect and unwavering ethics. Men often admired her beauty, drawn to her striking features and poise, but she had always prided herself on being more than just a pretty face. In her two years of practice, she had built a reputation as a formidable advocate in the courtroom. Her mother's meticulous planning had influenced her, but Vani had forged her own path, guided by principles that often stood in stark contrast to the life her mother had led.

As she approached the entrance, Vani recalled the threats from Vikram that had driven her to this moment. She was about to meet Aryan, a man tangled in a world she had long tried to distance herself from, yet here she was, representing him at Vikram's behest. The thought made her stomach churn, but she reminded herself that this was a means to an end—a way to protect her mother.

Inside, the air was thick with tension and a sense of despair. The guards eyed her with suspicion as she moved through the labyrinthine hallways, each step echoing off the concrete floors. She clutched her briefcase tightly, knowing that this meeting could change everything.

Finally, she was ushered into a dimly lit visitation room. The heavy steel door clanged shut behind her, and her pulse quickened. Aryan sat at the far end of the table, his dark hair slightly tousled and his expression unreadable. There was a dangerous allure to him, an intensity that was both intriguing and unsettling.

Aryan had seen a photo of Vani once in the newspaper, when her mom was being interviewed by the media regarding his case.

"Ms. Malhotra," he greeted, his voice smooth but laced with curiosity. "I didn't expect to see you here." "Neither did I," Vani replied, taking a seat across from him. She tried to maintain her composure, but she could feel the weight of his gaze, piercing and assessing.

She took a deep breath, her purpose clear. "I'm here to discuss your case. I'll be representing you in court, as part of a… agreement." The words felt heavy in her mouth.

"A deal with Vikram?" he asked, arching an eyebrow. "You know what you're getting into, right?"

"I do," she said firmly, meeting his gaze head-on. "But I also believe in justice, and I want to understand your side of the story. We'll need to go over some paperwork."

He leaned back, his demeanour shifting slightly, as if weighing her words. "You know this is dangerous territory, don't you? You're stepping into a world that could swallow you whole."

"I'm aware," Vani replied, her voice steady. "But I can handle it. I've dealt with tough cases before."

Aryan studied her for a moment, an unreadable expression on his face. "You're not like your mother," he finally said. "I can see that."

Vani felt a spark of defiance. "I'm not my mother, and I won't make the same mistakes she did. I'm here to help you, but I need your cooperation." She pulled out the documents, sliding them across the table. "I'll need your signature on these court papers to move forward."

He picked up the pen, his fingers brushing against the paper as he signed. "You really think you can take down the cops? They have a strong case against me." he asked, scepticism lacing his voice.

"I'm not trying to take them down," Vani replied, her resolve unwavering. "I'm trying to protect my mother and get you a fair trial. There's a difference."

As Aryan signed the last document, he looked up, a flicker of respect passing between them. "You're brave, Vani. I'll give you that. Just be careful. Vikram doesn't play by the rules."

She nodded, knowing the truth in his words. "I'll be careful. But you need to trust me. We can work together to get you out of here."

In that moment, Vani felt an unexpected connection—a shared understanding of the darkness they were both trying to navigate. Aryan might be a man of crime, but she sensed there was more to him than what met the eye.

Over the next few days, Vani and Aryan's meetings became a sanctuary amidst the chaos that surrounded them. Each visit stripped away the layers of preconceived notions, revealing the man beneath the criminal façade. The prison walls, once a symbol of confinement and darkness, transformed into a space where they exchanged stories and aspirations.

Vani arrived each time armed with legal documents, but she found herself increasingly drawn to Aryan's narrative. He was kind, thoughtful, and surprisingly articulate. Their conversations flowed effortlessly, peppered with laughter and moments of deep reflection. Aryan's demeanour was far removed from the hardened criminal image that Vikram had painted.

"People see me as a monster," he admitted one afternoon, his expression serious as they sat across from each other. "But I'm not. I made choices—bad choices—out of desperation. It wasn't the life I wanted."

Vani listened intently; her pen poised above her notepad. "Tell me about your past, Aryan. The real you. I need to build a defence that shows the judge who you truly are."

He hesitated for a moment, as if searching for the right words. "I grew up in a loving family. My parents worked hard to give me a good education. I had dreams of a good job—I even worked for an airline for a while. But then… life happened."

He paused, looking out the small window, lost in thought. "I tried to build a life for myself, but I fell into a trap. Friends I trusted pulled me into their world, and before I knew it, I was in too deep. I never wanted this life."

Vani felt her heart ache for him. She had always believed that people were shaped by their choices, but hearing Aryan's story revealed a harsh truth: sometimes, circumstances could dictate those choices. "What do you want now?" she asked gently, trying to connect with the man who sat before her.

"I want to change," he replied, his eyes earnest. "I want to help others who are struggling like I did. If I can show the judge that I'm not just a criminal but a man who wants redemption, maybe I can prove I'm worthy of a second chance."

With every meeting, Vani gathered fragments of Aryan's life, crafting a defence that would highlight his humanity. She learned about his love for animals, his volunteer work at a local shelter before his downfall, and his desire to mentor at-risk youth. Each revelation painted a picture of a man who had strayed but was now determined to find his way back.

As they collaborated on the defence statement, Vani's admiration for Aryan grew. He was not the cold, calculating criminal she had envisioned; instead, he was someone who had made mistakes and was deeply remorseful. The more she listened, the more she believed in his potential for change.

"Vani," he said one day, his voice softening, "thank you for believing in me. It means more than you know."

She smiled, the warmth of his words wrapping around her like a comforting blanket. "Everyone deserves a chance to prove they can change, Aryan. You're not your past."

As the days turned into weeks, their bond deepened. Vani found herself drawn to his strength and vulnerability; qualities that made him even more compelling. He had a way of making her feel heard, respected, and valued—a rare connection that ignited something within her.

With each meeting, Aryan's resolve to change inspired her own determination. She was no longer just fighting for her mother's safety; she was also fighting for Aryan's redemption and the chance to rewrite their stories.

The days in prison felt interminable for Aryan, each hour stretching into an eternity of regret and longing. But with Vani's visits, time took on a different hue. Her presence transformed the bleak, grey walls into something more vibrant, almost hopeful. He found himself counting the days until their next meeting, eagerly awaiting her laughter and the light in her eyes.

Vani was everything he admired: beautiful, intelligent, and fiercely determined. With every conversation, Aryan felt the barriers he had built around his heart begin to crumble. He was drawn to her kindness, her unwavering belief in him, and the way she listened without judgment. Those moments spent together were his only solace amid the despair of incarceration.

One particularly sombre day, as Aryan recounted the darkest moment of his past—the night he had pulled the trigger and taken a life—his voice cracked under the weight of his emotions. Tears streamed down his face, and he felt the world closing in on him. The guilt was overwhelming, and for a fleeting moment, he thought he might drown in it.

Vani, sensing the weight of his despair, reached across the table, her fingers brushing against Aryan's. The touch was electric, sending a jolt through him, awakening a warmth he thought he had lost forever. "Aryan," she said softly, her voice a tender melody amid the chaos of his thoughts, "you're not alone in this."

In a moment that felt both spontaneous and inevitable, she stood up, stepping closer to him, and wrapped her arms around him in a tight embrace. The world outside the prison walls faded away, and all that remained was the intoxicating warmth of her body against his. He felt her heartbeat, a steady rhythm that grounded him, reminding him that there was still life, still hope.

As Aryan buried his face in her shoulder, he was overwhelmed by the flood of emotion that broke free. He sobbed, raw and unfiltered, each tremor of his body releasing the pent-up anguish he had been holding inside. "I'm so sorry," he choked out, the words muffled against her fabric. "I never wanted this life."

Vani held him tighter, her arms like a sanctuary, enveloping him in a cocoon of safety.
"You're not defined by your past, Aryan," she murmured, her breath warm against his ear. "You're stronger than this pain. I'm here for you, always."

As they pulled back, their eyes locked, and an unspoken understanding enveloped them like a warm embrace. In that moment, surrounded by the sterile environment of the prison, Aryan felt a powerful realization wash over him: he had fallen for her, deeper than he had ever thought possible.

"Vani," he said, his voice steady despite the tears that still glistened on his cheeks, "I love you. I want to get out of here, and I want to marry you. I want to take care of you and show you how grateful I am for everything you've done for me."

Vani's eyes widened in surprise, a rush of emotions cascading through her. Her heart raced, caught between shock and joy. "I… I've started to love you too,

Aryan," she admitted, her voice trembling with sincerity. "I didn't know how to say it, but I do."

The air around them crackled with the electricity of their confessions. Aryan took her hands in his, their fingers interlacing perfectly, as if they were always meant to be together. "Then let's promise each other," he said, a determined glint in his eye. "When I get out, we'll start a new life. A life that's ours—free from all this chaos."

Tears of joy shimmered in Vani's eyes, and she squeezed his hands tightly, feeling the strength of his resolve. "Yes! I want that too," she breathed, her heart soaring. "We'll face whatever comes our way, together."

In a moment that felt suspended in time, they leaned in closer, the air between them crackling with anticipation. Their lips met in a kiss that was both tender and electric, a fusion of longing and desperation that sent shivers down Aryan's spine. It was more than just a kiss; it was a promise, a declaration of everything unspoken yet deeply felt.

As their mouths moved together, the world around them dissolved into a blur. The cold, sterile walls of the prison melted away, replaced by an intoxicating warmth that enveloped them both. Aryan could taste the salt of their tears mingled with the sweetness of hope, a reminder that love could blossom even in the bleakest of places.

Vani's hands found their way to Aryan's face, her fingers cradling him as if he were the most precious thing in the world. Every brush of her skin ignited a fire within him, fuelling his resolve to reclaim his future. He deepened the kiss, pouring all his emotions into that single moment—his gratitude, his fear, his yearning.

As they kissed, the rhythm of their hearts synchronized, each thump echoing the promise of a shared life. Aryan pulled her closer, feeling the warmth of her body against his, a stark contrast to the cold reality outside. Time stood still as they surrendered to the connection that enveloped them, losing themselves in the magic of the moment.

Just as they pulled away, they heard a laugh behind them. The constable on duty, who had been pretending to mind his own business, couldn't help himself. He whistled loudly, a mischievous grin spreading across his face. "Well, that's one for the books! Love in a prison? Never thought I'd see the day!"

Vani and Aryan broke into a fit of laughter, the tension in the room dissipating. Aryan wiped his tears, feeling lighter, almost liberated by the shared joy. He couldn't help but smile at the absurdity of it all—the unlikely romance blooming in the starkest of places.

In that moment, surrounded by laughter and hope, Aryan felt a renewed sense of purpose. Vani was his light, guiding him through the darkness. With Vani's love as his armour, he would face every obstacle, conquer every fear, and turn their shared despair into a radiant love story that would rise above the ashes of their struggles. Their hearts beat in sync, a powerful rhythm promising that, no matter how dark the night, they would emerge into the light, hand in hand.

CHAPTER 6
FREEDOM, LOVE, & FRIENDSHIP

The air in the courtroom was thick with tension as Vani prepared for the most crucial day of her career. She could feel the weight of expectation pressing down on her, but determination coursed through her veins. This was not just a trial for Aryan; it was a trial for his very future—and, in many ways, her own.

As she stood at the front of the room, she could see the stern faces of the judge and jury, the opposing counsel smirking with confidence, and Aryan sitting quietly at the defendant's table, his expression a mixture of hope and apprehension. Vani took a deep breath, adjusting her notes, and steeled herself for what lay ahead.

The trial began with the usual formalities, but soon the atmosphere turned combative. The opposition lawyer, a seasoned veteran with a reputation for intimidation, wasted no time in attacking Vani's credibility. "Ladies and gentlemen," he began, his voice dripping with disdain, "we have a young lawyer here who seems to be wasting the court's precious time. After all, her mother is in the hospital—perhaps due to her own questionable dealings. What can we expect from her but a desperate attempt to save her own skin?"

Gasps rippled through the courtroom, and Vani's blood boiled. She could feel the heat rising to her cheeks, but she refused to let him undermine her. Gathering her composure, she shot back, "Your Honor, I would like to remind the court that personal attacks are irrelevant to the case at hand. This trial is about Aryan, not my mother!"

Her voice rang out with conviction, silencing the courtroom. The opposing lawyer was momentarily taken aback, his smirk faltering.

"Furthermore," Vani continued, her tone sharp and unwavering, "to suggest that my mother's situation reflects on my ability to defend Aryan is not only unfair but also an insult to the legal system. I stand here representing my client based on facts and the merit of his character."

She could see the judge nod slightly, a hint of approval in his eyes. Vani's heart raced as she pushed forward, presenting the evidence she had meticulously gathered. "Aryan comes from a good family. He was once a promising young man, working hard in the airline industry. He did not choose this life; it chose him due to circumstances beyond his control. But he is not the criminal you make him out to be."

As she spoke, she glanced at Aryan, whose eyes glistened with a mix of admiration and gratitude. This was their fight, and she was determined to show the world the man he truly was.

Vani pulled up photographs and documents on the screen behind her, illustrating Aryan's past—his family, his education, and the charity work he had done before falling into a web of crime. "This is not the profile of a monster," she argued passionately. "This is a man who has recognized his mistakes and wants to make amends. He deserves a chance at redemption, not condemnation."

The courtroom was silent, hanging on her every word. She could see some members of the jury nodding, and for a fleeting moment, hope blossomed within her.

Then came the critical moment—the opposing lawyer, flustered but still desperate, attempted to pivot back to the incident that had led to Aryan's arrest. "Let's not forget the serious accusations against him. He was implicated in the shooting of a businessman outside his office. What about that?"

Vani seized the opportunity, her voice rising above the murmurs. "Your Honor, there is no evidence connecting Aryan to that incident! He was nowhere near the scene at the time of the shooting. We have alibis and witnesses ready to testify. This isn't about guilt; it's about innocence!"

The courtroom fell silent, and Vani stepped back, her heart racing. She had fought with everything she had, pouring her soul into her defence. As she looked over at Aryan, she saw him staring back, a silent acknowledgment passing between them.

The judge called for a recess, and Vani felt a wave of exhaustion wash over her. But amidst the fatigue, she also felt a flicker of hope—a hope that their fight might finally lead to Aryan's freedom, which they both desperately sought.

As Vani stepped back into the courtroom, a renewed sense of determination surged within her. She had come too far to back down now. The evidence she had meticulously gathered was about to play a pivotal role in Aryan's defence.

With a deep breath, she presented the flight tickets and hotel bookings that confirmed Aryan's whereabouts on the day of the shooting. "Your Honor," she said, her voice steady and unwavering, "the prosecution's case hinges entirely on the idea that my client was present at the scene of the crime. However, I have irrefutable proof that he was out of town, as these documents clearly illustrate."

She laid the flight tickets and hotel bookings on the table for the judge to see, ensuring that every juror had a clear view. The courtroom buzzed with whispers as people processed the implications of her evidence.

"I also have a witness who can confirm Aryan's presence at the airport on the day in question," Vani continued, calling her next witness to the stand—an employee from the airport who worked at the check-in counter.

The witness, a young woman with a confident demeanour, took the stand. "Yes, I remember Aryan very well," she said, glancing at him with a friendly smile. "He checked in for his flight that morning. I was working at the counter, and he was polite and engaging."

Vani leaned forward, encouraging her to elaborate. "Can you confirm the time of his check-in?"

The employee nodded. "Absolutely. He checked in at around 9:00 AM, well before the incident occurred. I remember it clearly because he had a unique travel bag."

As she spoke, Vani could see the jury's expressions shift from scepticism to intrigue. The narrative was changing, and she could sense it.

Once the employee finished, Vani called another witness—a hotel clerk who verified Aryan's stay. "He checked in on the evening prior and checked out the morning after the incident," the clerk confirmed. "I remember him very well ma'am; how can I forget? He was kind enough to tip all the staff at the hotel while leaving."

As the evidence piled up, Vani felt the tide turning in their favour. She glanced at Aryan, who sat with a mix of hope and anxiety etched on his face. This was their moment.

With the prosecution scrambling to refute her evidence, Vani seized the opportunity. "Given the lack of credible evidence tying Aryan to this crime, I request the court to dismiss the case immediately," she stated boldly. "If that is not possible, I implore you to consider granting him bail. He poses no flight risk and is eager to prove his innocence."

The judge leaned back in his chair, contemplating her request. The courtroom held its breath, the tension palpable.

After a few moments that felt like an eternity, the judge spoke. "I have considered the evidence presented and the testimonies given. While the prosecution has presented serious allegations, the defence has shown substantial evidence of Aryan's alibi. Therefore, I am inclined to grant bail, pending further investigations."

Relief washed over Vani, and she caught Aryan's eye. He smiled, a genuine expression of gratitude and hope lighting up his features. This was a significant victory, and they were one step closer to justice.

As the gavel sounded, marking the end of the day's proceedings, Vani felt a rush of adrenaline. The courtroom emptied, but Aryan remained, a look of disbelief on his face.

"Thank you, Vani," he said, his voice thick with emotion. "You saved me today."

Without a second thought, Vani stepped forward, wrapping her arms around him tightly. Aryan embraced her back, holding her as if she were his lifeline. In that moment, they felt the world fade away—just the two of them, encapsulated in their own bubble of relief and joy.

As they pulled back slightly, their eyes locked, and without hesitation, they leaned in and shared a passionate kiss, a promise of support and affection that dimmed the chaos surrounding them.

In the weeks that followed, Vani and Aryan didn't waste any time. Fuelled by an unshakeable sense of hope and a love that had flourished amidst the shadows of despair, they made a life-changing decision. They would marry.

The wedding was a simple yet intimate affair, held in a small, unassuming courtroom that felt more like a sanctuary than a place of law. The day was bathed in a soft glow as sunlight streamed through the windows, casting a warm hue over everything. Vani wore a stunning red dress that clung to her form, a vibrant symbol of their fiery love and the passion that had ignited between them. As she entered the room, Aryan's breath caught in his throat. In that moment, she radiated strength and beauty, her confidence shining brighter than the fabric that adorned her.

Surrounded by a handful of close friends who had stood by them through the chaos, the atmosphere was thick with emotion. Laughter mingled with nervous anticipation as they gathered in support, creating an intimate cocoon of warmth. Each friend exchanged knowing smiles, their eyes glistening with tears of joy for the couple who had fought so hard to find their way back to each other.

As they stood before the officiant, the world outside faded into a blur, and time seemed to stretch infinitely. Vani's heart raced as Aryan looked at her, his gaze filled with an intensity that made her feel like the only person in the universe. Each vow exchanged felt like a weight being lifted, the burdens of their past slowly dissolving into the promise of a brighter future. "I will stand by you, through every storm," Aryan pledged, his voice steady yet thick with emotion, the sincerity of his words echoing in the small room.

Vani's heart swelled as she reciprocated, "I choose you, Aryan, now and forever." Their voices intertwined, creating a symphony of love that enveloped them. The moment hung suspended in time, charged with the unspoken understanding that they had both transformed from their past selves into something beautiful together.

As they sealed their vows with a kiss, the kiss lingered longer than they had intended, a sweet mingling of passion and promise. The warmth of Aryan's lips against hers ignited a fire within her, a reminder that love could blossom even in the darkest of times. Around them, their friends erupted in applause, their joy palpable, but all Aryan and Vani could see was each other—their hearts beating in sync, a rhythm of hope and determination.

When they finally pulled away, Aryan cupped her face in his hands, his eyes searching hers. "This is just the beginning, my love," he whispered, his voice a tender caress that sent shivers down her spine. In that moment, they left behind the weight of their past and stepped boldly into their future, hand in hand, ready to face whatever life threw their way.

After the ceremony, Vani and Aryan rented a cozy apartment in a tranquil neighbourhood, a serene refuge from the chaos that had defined their lives for so long. The air felt lighter here, imbued with the scent of fresh paint and the promise of new beginnings. Sunlight poured through the large windows, illuminating the space and casting a warm glow over their shared dreams.

In this sanctuary, they created a tapestry of little moments that wove their hearts closer together. Cooking together became a cherished ritual, the kitchen filled with the sounds of laughter and playful banter as they experimented with new recipes. Flour dusted their hands, and the aroma of spices danced in the air, mingling with the sweet sound of Vani's laughter as

Aryan attempted to flip pancakes, only for them to land in a lopsided heap.

Late into the night, they shared stories, their voices hushed yet filled with warmth as they recounted their pasts—each revelation a step toward healing. Vani spoke of her dreams, the childhood aspirations that had been overshadowed by her responsibilities, while Aryan shared the journey that had led him to the shadows and, ultimately, back to the light. Each story drew them closer, building a foundation of trust and understanding.

Vani was determined to craft a life filled with peace and happiness, a life that would help them both heal from the scars of their pasts. She filled their home with little touches of warmth—soft blankets draped over the couch, colourful cushions, and small plants that thrived in the sunlight.

In the quiet moments, when the world outside faded away, Aryan would often pull Vani close, wrapping his arms around her as they watched the sunset paint the sky in hues of gold and crimson. "I never thought I could be this happy," he would whisper, his voice filled with awe. Vani would smile, her heart swelling with warmth, knowing they had both fought so hard to reach this point.

Their love flourished in this nurturing environment, blossoming like the flowers Vani tended to on their small balcony.

On the professional front, Vani's fame skyrocketed after securing Aryan's bail. The legal community buzzed with admiration for her fierce advocacy and unwavering belief in her client. Journalists flocked to interview her, eager to hear the story of the young lawyer who had taken on the odds and won. The very next hearing, the judge dismissed the case against Aryan entirely, declaring him not guilty. The courtroom erupted in cheers, but for Vani and Aryan, it was a moment of relief and joy.

As the news spread, the couple celebrated this victory together, a fresh start filled with possibility. Vani was no longer just Mrs. Malhotra's daughter; she was Mrs. Vani Aryan Khan, a lawyer who had carved her own path, who had fought not just for Aryan's freedom, but for her own life along with her mothers.

As the weeks passed, Vani and Aryan's happiness blossomed with the arrival of their baby boy, Aarav. The little one filled their home with laughter and joy, and they cherished every moment of parenthood. Vani's mother doted on her grandson, showering him with gifts and affection, bringing warmth and light into their lives. Yet, beneath the surface of this bliss, Aryan felt a growing tension gnawing at him.

Despite the joy of fatherhood, Aryan was deeply troubled. The happiness of cradling his newborn son often collided with the dark remnants of his past, creating a whirlwind of emotions that left him feeling torn. After his release from jail, he had made every effort to leave that life behind.

One night, he found himself in a dimly lit bar, the kind of place that whispered secrets and echoes of old loyalties. He had approached Vikram, the notorious don who had once been both his mentor and his prison. The air crackled with tension as he walked in, the murmurs of old gang members fading into silence. Aryan felt like a ghost in a place that once felt like home, but this time, he was there to sever ties.

"Vikram," he began, his voice steady yet laced with apprehension. "I need to walk away. I can't drag my family into this anymore." The don regarded him with a mix of amusement and irritation. The room felt charged, as if the very walls were holding their breath.

Vikram leaned back, a sardonic smile creeping across his face. "You think you can just leave, Aryan? You know what we do to those who try to cut ties."

Aryan's heart raced, but he held his ground. "I won't betray any of your secrets. I promise. But I need a chance at a normal life—for my son, for Vani. I'm done with the shadows."

The silence hung heavy, a palpable weight of uncertainty. Finally, Vikram, begrudgingly impressed by Aryan's resolve, leaned forward. "Fine. I'll let you go, but know this: the shadows never truly leave you. One misstep, and I'll come for you."

As Aryan walked out, a mixture of relief and dread washed over him. The weight of his decision pressed down like a shroud. But as he stepped into the night, the chill of reality hit him—severing ties with the underworld was one thing; rebuilding his life was another. The shadows of his past loomed larger than ever, making it nearly impossible for him to secure a respectable job.

Weeks turned into months, and each rejection weighed heavily on Aryan's heart, dragging him deeper into a pit of despair. He was resolute in his mission to provide for his family, yet as he scoured job listings and attended interview after interview, the same grim fate awaited him. Fear and prejudice loomed like dark clouds, casting shadows over every hopeful conversation.

No one wanted to hire a man with a criminal record, no matter how sincere his intentions or how much he emphasized his desire for change. Each "thank you for your interest, but..." felt like a dagger to his resolve. The humiliation and frustration piled up, suffocating him, making him question his worth and his choices.

At home, Vani noticed the toll it was taking. The once-vibrant spark in Aryan's eyes had dimmed, replaced by a lingering sadness that echoed in their small apartment. He would sit in silence, staring out the window as if searching for answers in the world beyond. Vani's heart ached to see him like this; she could feel the weight of his struggles pressing down on them both.

One evening, as the sun dipped below the horizon, painting the sky in hues of orange and pink, Vani reached for Aryan's hand. "We'll get through this together," she said softly, her voice steady but laced with concern. "You're so much more than your past. I believe in you."

Aryan squeezed her hand, but the flicker of hope was dimmed by the relentless tide of negativity that engulfed him. "I wish I could believe that," he admitted, his voice barely above a whisper. "But every door I try to open just slams shut in my face."

That night, after Vani had gone to bed, Aryan found himself alone with his thoughts, the shadows of his past creeping closer. He felt trapped between two worlds—the life he had left behind and the future he desperately wanted to build.

Vani was working tirelessly, dedicating herself to cases that championed the rights of the poor and innocent. Every day, she poured her heart and soul into her work, advocating for those who had been wronged by a system that often overlooked them. Yet, despite her passion and commitment, her earnings were limited, a harsh reality that weighed heavily on her.

She was steadfast in her principles, refusing to compromise her ethics by representing clients who didn't align with her values. To her, every case was more than just a pay check; it was a chance to make a real difference in someone's life. But as much as she loved her work, the financial strain they faced loomed like a dark cloud over their home.

The couple had once envisioned a life filled with laughter and light, but with every passing week, the bills piled up. Vani would sit at their modest kitchen table, papers spread out in front of her, the flickering candlelight casting long shadows across her tired face. Despite the warmth of the moment, she felt the chill of worry creeping in.

"Aryan, I'm doing everything I can," she'd say, her voice steady but laced with concern. "I can take on more cases, maybe even work late into the night. I just need to find a way to bring in more income."

Aryan watched her, frustration swelling within him. He wanted nothing more than to relieve her burden, but he felt trapped.

Every time Aryan looked at his son, Aarav, a wave of desperation washed over him. The innocent gaze of his child held so much promise, yet Aryan couldn't shake the gnawing fear of what kind of life he could truly provide. The shadows of his past loomed large, threatening to encroach upon the bright future he envisioned for his family.

What would happen if their neighbours discovered the truth about him? Would they see him as nothing more than a criminal, a failure? The thought of Aarav facing judgment, burdened by the stigma of his father's mistakes, twisted painfully in Aryan's gut. Each smile from his son felt like a reminder of the weight of responsibility he carried—a weight that felt heavier by the day.

As if fate conspired to push him further, Vani announced her pregnancy once again. The news initially filled him with joy, a hope for their family's future. Yet, as he absorbed the reality of bringing another life into the world, the anxiety crept back in. Another little boy, another mouth to feed, and with it, the pressure to secure a stable income intensified.

With every flutter of Vani's belly, Aryan felt the stakes rising. He longed to be a father who could provide, who could offer his children a life free from the chains of his past. But with each passing day, as the bills piled up and the job rejections continued, he felt increasingly trapped.

Vani, radiant and glowing, often caught him lost in thought. "Aryan, what's wrong?" she would ask, concern etching her features. "We'll figure this out together."

"I know, I just—" His voice would falter, the weight of unfulfilled promises hanging heavily in the air. "I want to give you and the boys everything you deserve. I don't want you to ever feel like you have to struggle."

"Then let's keep fighting," she would say, her resolve unwavering. "You've come so far already. Don't lose hope."

But hope felt fragile, like a thread ready to snap under pressure. The mounting fear of the past catching up with him loomed larger than ever. How could he protect his family when the world seemed determined to pull them back into the shadows?

Each evening, as he held Aarav close, Aryan would whisper promises into the boy's soft hair. "I'll find a way, I promise. I'll do whatever it takes to make our life better." But deep down, he worried that those promises might be as fragile as the hope they clung to.

With Vani expecting their second child, he couldn't shake the feeling that time was running out. He needed to act—to reclaim his life and secure a future for them all.

One evening, as Vani gently tucked their two boys into bed, Aryan sat alone at the kitchen table, the weight of uncertainty pressing down on him. The soft hum of the night surrounded him, punctuated only by the faint sounds of his children settling into sleep. His phone lay in front of him, displaying a list of contacts that felt like lifelines, yet he hesitated.

He took a deep breath, his heart racing as he scrolled through names. Memories flooded back—laughter, camaraderie, late-night study sessions. But the shadows of his past loomed large, whispering doubts in his mind. Would Carl still see him as the ambitious young man he once was, or only as the man who had fallen from grace?

After a moment of self-reflection, Aryan steeled his resolve. He tapped Carl's name and pressed the call button. The phone rang, each tone echoing his mounting anxiety. What if Carl rejected him? What if the conversation went south?

"Hello?" Carl's familiar voice broke through the tension.

"Hey, Carl! It's Aryan," he said, trying to keep his voice steady.

"Aryan! Wow, it's been ages. How have you been?" Carl replied, genuine warmth in his tone.

"It's a long story," Aryan began, feeling the weight of the years, they had lost touch. "I really need your help, man. I'm looking for work, and I thought maybe you could point me in the right direction?"

Carl was silent for a moment, and Aryan could sense the surprise and perhaps concern. "Yeah, sure. I can help. But… things haven't been easy for you, have they?"

"No, they haven't. I'm trying to change, Carl. I just want to be a good husband and father. I don't want to go back to that life."

"I get it. Listen, I might have a lead for you. One of my friends, Chetan, is the CEO of a huge shipping corporation overseas. He's always looking for reliable people, and I'm pretty sure he could help you out."

Aryan felt a flicker of hope. "Really? You think he'd be willing to take me on?"

"Absolutely. Let me make a call to him right now and see what I can do. I'll vouch for you, Aryan. Just give me a minute."

As Carl's voice faded, Aryan's heart raced with anticipation. This could be the opportunity he had been waiting for.

A few moments later, Carl returned. "Chetan's interested in talking to you. He has asked us to come visit. Can you meet him?"

"Yes, I'll be there!" Aryan replied, his voice filled with gratitude. "Thank you so much, Carl. This means everything to me."

After hanging up, Aryan felt a wave of relief wash over him. Finally, there was a glimmer of hope on the horizon. As he looked at Vani and Aarav, he resolved to do whatever it took to secure their future. He crossed his fingers, hoping that Carl's friend Chetan would provide the support he so desperately needed. As he moved into the living room, Aryan's mind whirred with possibilities. What if Chetan could offer him a job? What if this was the turning point, he had been praying for? The thought filled him with a sense of purpose that he hadn't felt in ages.

That night, as they sat together on the couch, Vani sensed his restlessness. "What's on your mind?" she asked, her voice gentle yet probing.

"I spoke with Carl today. He's going to introduce me to his friend Chetan," Aryan said, his voice barely above a whisper.

Her eyes sparkled with encouragement. "That's great news! You've worked so hard for this moment. I know you'll impress him."

"I hope so," he replied, running a hand through his hair in a gesture of anxiety. "But what if he doesn't look past my past? What if he sees me only as that man who was arrested?"

Vani reached for his hand, squeezing it tightly. "You are not defined by your past, Aryan. You are a loving husband and father. You're fighting for us, and that speaks volumes. Just be yourself."

Her words wrapped around him like a warm embrace, giving him strength. "I'm just scared that I'll let you down," he admitted, vulnerability creeping into his tone.

"You could never let us down. Remember, we're in this together," she assured him, her eyes locking onto his with unwavering conviction. "Whatever happens, we'll figure it out."

Saying that, she slept peacefully, and Aryan continued thinking about the upcoming meeting with Carl's friend that was probably going to define his future.

This is what resulted in that fateful morning, where the two old friends were re-united. It was Karma's plan that they would help each other out of the problem's they were stuck in.

CHAPTER 7
THE ROAD TO REDEMPTION

After the meeting with Chetan, Aryan settled into the apartment that had been provided for him. But as he unpacked, his thoughts were consumed by the escalating situation at the warehouse. Outside, the clamour of striking workers reached a crescendo, fuelled by the fervent rhetoric of their union leader, John—a man known for his fiery speeches and deep-seated animosity toward Chetan and the corporation.

Chetan had entrusted Aryan with a monumental task: to quell the unrest among the workers and restore a semblance of order. Aryan, aware of his own past and the shadows that loomed over him, understood the gravity of this responsibility. He was no stranger to conflict, having navigated the treacherous waters of the underworld. But now, he was on the other side of the law, fighting for redemption in a world that had once cast him aside.

Yet there was more to the story. Carl had filled him in on the whispers of danger surrounding Chetan and his family—death threats that loomed like storm clouds, threatening to cast a dark shadow over their lives. Aryan felt a fierce determination ignite within him. Not only did he need to resolve the strike, but he also had to ensure the safety of Chetan and his family.

As the new operations head of the facility, Aryan felt the weight of the task ahead. Chetan had entrusted him with the responsibility to resolve the escalating strike. There were rumours of John manipulating the workers for his gain, and Aryan was determined to put a stop to it.

With resolve steeling his heart, Aryan made his way to the warehouse, the tension in the air palpable. As he entered, the sight before him was chaotic: workers shouted, holding placards demanding justice, while John stood at the forefront, orchestrating the unrest with a calculated flair.

"Hey, everyone! Let's calm down!" Aryan called, trying to project authority over the rising din. "I'm Aryan, the new operations head. I'm here to listen and find a way to resolve this situation."

John's eyes narrowed, a sly grin creeping across his face. "And why should we listen to you, Aryan? You think you can just waltz in here and fix everything? You don't know anything about our struggles!"

Aryan approached the crowd, undeterred by John's hostile demeanour. "I understand you're upset, and I want to hear your concerns. But we need to talk this out."

Before he could continue, John stepped closer, a menacing presence. "You think you can come here and threaten me? This is our fight, and I won't let you take that away from us."

In a split second, John pushed Aryan, a challenge ringing in the air like a thunderclap. The workers fell silent, tension coiling around them as they sensed the impending clash. Aryan's instincts kicked in, honed by years of navigating volatile situations. With a swift motion, he seized John's wrist, twisting it with a precision that spoke of his past experiences in confrontations.

The moment felt electric, the air thick with anticipation. Aryan thrust John against a nearby post, the impact reverberating through the crowd. John's eyes widened in shock; the bravado momentarily stripped away as he realized the strength of Aryan's grip. Gasps erupted from the onlookers, their faces painted with a mix of surprise and fear.

"Enough!" Aryan's voice rang out, steady and commanding, cutting through the chaos like a blade. His gaze locked onto John's, fierce and unwavering. The crowd shifted, the dynamic now altered; they were no longer just spectators but witnesses to a power struggle unfolding before them.

Aryan's heart raced, adrenaline surging through him. "I'm not your enemy," he declared, his tone firm yet measured. "I'm here to work with you. Let me explain." The gravity of the moment hung heavily in the air; the workers now transfixed by Aryan's determination.

As he released John, the tension didn't dissipate; instead, it crackled like a live wire. Aryan stepped back, maintaining an authoritative presence while gauging the crowd's reaction. "If you agree to resume work immediately," he continued, his voice resonating with conviction, "I'll ensure you're compensated for the days lost in this unnecessary strike. We all have families to feed. I want to work alongside you, like one of you, to solve these issues together."

John's expression twisted into a scowl, fury igniting in his eyes as he struggled to regain his composure. "You think a few days of pay will make us forget what we're fighting for? We're not pawns in your game!" he retorted, desperation creeping into his voice.

But Aryan stood tall, unwavering. “I’m not asking you to forget,” he countered, his voice rich with empathy. “I’m asking for your trust. We can’t create a better workplace if we’re at each other’s throats. Let’s end this strike and find common ground.”

The workers exchanged glances, uncertainty flickering across their faces. Slowly, the tension began to shift. Aryan took a deep breath, sensing the moment hanging in the balance.

“Together, we can build a better environment,” he continued, his sincerity cutting through the hostility. “I need your voices to be heard, but we can only do that if we’re working side by side. Trust me—give me this opportunity, and I won’t let you down.”

As silence fell over the crowd, John’s expression shifted from anger to contemplation. He knew he had lost some control of the situation. Aryan had stepped up, showing strength and conviction that the workers could rally behind.

Finally, one of the workers spoke up. “Let’s hear him out. We’ve been fighting for our rights long enough. Maybe it’s time to see if he really means what he says.”

Aryan spent the entire day immersed in the workers' grievances, his heart heavy with their frustrations and fears. The atmosphere in the warehouse was charged with tension, each complaint layered with a sense of betrayal. As he listened, he could see the anxiety etched on their faces—lines of worry deepened by the uncertainty of their futures.

John, the cunning agitator, had been weaving a web of lies, skilfully manipulating the workers' emotions. He claimed that the foreign company had seized their land, exploiting it for profit while disregarding the very people who had toiled on it for generations. "They're just here to drain us dry," one worker exclaimed, his voice trembling with anger. "Once they've taken everything, they'll leave us with nothing!"

John had spun this narrative into a powerful rhetoric, painting a picture of an impending doom that loomed over the community like a dark cloud. He warned the workers that once the company had extracted all it could, it would abandon them, leaving families jobless and desperate, their livelihoods shattered. "We will be left with empty pockets and broken dreams!" he had lied to them.

Aryan felt a surge of frustration rise within him. He could see how John's words had taken root, sowing seeds of distrust and fear among the workers. They were vulnerable, and John was exploiting that vulnerability for his own gain. Aryan's resolve hardened; he knew he had to dismantle this narrative.

John couldn't just be a quiet spectator. He realized he had to say something, or else Aryan would convince the workers to call off the strike.

John further incited the workers, his voice rising with fervour as he painted an enticing picture of a brighter future. "I know a local company," he declared, eyes gleaming with deceit, "one that's ready to take over our operations the moment we can drive this foreign firm out! They've promised to pay us higher wages, to treat us like the workers we deserve to be!"

His words hung in the air like a siren's call, striking a chord in the hearts of the already anxious labourers. Desperation danced in their eyes as they clung to the hope of better pay and improved conditions. John's cunning rhetoric fed their fears, twisting the truth to serve his agenda. "This foreign company is here to exploit us! They don't care about our families or our futures!" he shouted, his voice thick with conviction.

The workers erupted in a mix of anger and excitement, fuelled by John's manipulation. They gathered in tighter clusters, their conversations charged with a growing sense of rebellion. "We deserve better!" one voice cried out, echoing the sentiments of many. "If they won't give us what we deserve, let's show them we won't stand for it!"

As the crowd grew more animated, John sensed the tide turning in his favour. "A strike is our only option!" he proclaimed, raising his fist high, a gesture of defiance that resonated throughout the assembly. "We need to stand united and demand what is rightfully ours! If we make them feel our power, they'll have no choice but to listen!"

With each passing moment, Aryan felt the tension escalating. The once-familiar faces of the workers transformed into a sea of determined expressions, their anger palpable and their sense of solidarity burgeoning. The chant of "Strike! Strike!" began to ripple through the crowd, growing louder and more insistent, drowning out any attempts to reason with them.

Aryan's heart raced. He knew this was a crucial moment; the stakes were higher than ever. The strike would not only jeopardize their livelihoods but also threaten the fragile stability of the community. He had to act swiftly before the wave of unrest swept them all away.

Furious, Aryan confronted John, his voice rising above the growing unrest. "You're lying to them!" he shouted. "You need to leave this job—now!" Grabbing John by the collar, he pushed him away from the group, a clear show of authority.

The workers watched, a mix of fear and hope in their eyes. "I promise you," Aryan continued, addressing them directly, "if you end this strike, I'll speak with Chetan about increasing your pay. You deserve better than this manipulation!"

As tensions escalated, John leapt towards Aryan, trying to land a fist in his stomach. Aryan blocked him swiftly, and hurled him backwards. Aryan and John engaged in a brief but intense struggle. Aryan was no newbie to fights. Within seconds he had John pinned to the floor, blood trickling from his cut lips. Aryan's punch to John's face had stunned him and forced him to retreat, bruised and vengeful.

"You'll regret this," John snarled as he backed away, a threat hanging in the air.

With John finally out of the picture, Aryan turned to face the workers, a fierce resolve lighting up his eyes. "Let's get back to work! Together, we can make this right!" His voice rang out with confidence, cutting through the lingering tension in the air.

The workers, initially hesitant, began to feel a shift in the atmosphere. Aryan's determination sparked something in them—a flicker of hope that had been buried under layers of fear and manipulation. They exchanged glances, some nodding slowly, as Aryan's words settled in.

Encouraged by his leadership, they rallied, their spirits lifting as they realized they had someone who truly believed in them. "Yeah! Let's do it!" one worker shouted, followed by a chorus of agreement.

With a collective sense of purpose, they started to gather their tools and prepare to return to their tasks. The sounds of machinery began to hum again, filling the air with a newfound energy. Aryan moved among them, offering words of encouragement, his presence a reassuring anchor amidst the chaos they had just experienced.

However, the workers were not the only threat lurking in the shadows. As Aryan had suspected, the competitors John served were emboldened by his earlier success, resorting to more sinister tactics to target Chetan and his family.

One evening, as night cloaked the neighbourhood in darkness, a sudden chaos erupted. A flurry of stones rained down upon Chetan's home, shattering the tranquillity of the night. The sharp sound of glass splintering echoed through the halls, sending shards cascading to the ground like a cruel reminder of the lurking danger. Chetan and his family were jolted from their peace, hearts racing as they rushed to the windows, fear etched across their faces. The sight outside was harrowing; the air thick with tension, and the shadows seemed to shift ominously in the flickering streetlights.

The following week, as Chetan was returning from a meeting, back to the warehouse, an unnerving stillness enveloped the road. Aryan was driving the car, his instincts on high alert. Suddenly, the silence shattered as gunshots rang out, reverberating through the air like thunder. Bullets tore through the vehicle, narrowly missing Chetan's car and embedding themselves in the pavement, sending debris flying in all directions.

Chetan's heart raced as he instinctively ducked, adrenaline flooding his system. "Drive!" he shouted, his voice filled with urgency. Aryan reacted swiftly, slamming his foot on the accelerator. The car lurched forward, tires screeching as they sped away from the barrage. In the rearview mirror, Chetan caught a glimpse of the chaos behind them—figures retreating into the shadows, their malicious intent clear.

As they sped towards safety, the gravity of the situation weighed heavily on both men. The threats were becoming increasingly brazen, and they realized that they were not just fighting for their business but for their very lives. Chetan's mind raced as he considered the implications. He had built this company from the ground up, and now it felt as if everything was teetering on the edge of collapse.

Aryan, sensing the urgency, turned to Chetan, determination etched on his face. "We need to act fast. They're not going to stop until they get what they want."

Chetan nodded, a fierce resolve igniting within him. "We'll strengthen our security. I won't let fear dictate our lives. We'll confront this head-on."

Realizing that the situation had grown dire, Aryan knew immediate action was essential. Chetan needed armed security—an unyielding presence to protect him from those who sought to harm him. Aryan quickly orchestrated a plan, coordinating with local law enforcement and hiring private security to ensure Chetan's safety.

From that day forward, every time Chetan ventured outdoors, he was escorted by an armed convoy. Aryan took his position in the front jeep, eyes scanning the surroundings, alert for any sign of trouble. The second jeep followed closely, packed with security guards ready to spring into action at a moment's notice. Each journey was a meticulous operation; no detail was overlooked.

To further ensure their safety, Aryan implemented a rotating schedule for the security guards. This strategy was designed to eliminate any chance of information leaks regarding Chetan's travel plans. Each guard was briefed on strict protocols, and the teams were switched frequently, maintaining an ever-vigilant shield around Chetan.

On longer drives, Aryan took additional precautions. He arranged for a backup car to be stationed midway through their journey. This vehicle was to be used for a quick swap, ensuring that no one could track Chetan's movements. Every mile was mapped out, every potential threat considered.

As Aryan and Chetan continued to navigate their situation, a sense of unease crept into the air. They began to suspect that there was a mole within their organization—a leak that was feeding vital information to their competitors. The realization hit them hard: someone close to Chetan was betraying him, and the stakes had never been higher.

One evening, a security guard who had built a strong rapport with Chetan approached him with grave concern. "I've noticed something unusual," he said, lowering his voice as if the walls themselves had ears. "Your personal assistant has been leaving the premises frequently. He meets with an ex-union employee—John. They sit outside the gates for hours, chatting over cups of tea."

Chetan frowned, disbelief washing over him. "That's odd. I thought he was dedicated to the job. Why would he waste time with someone like John?"

Aryan's brow furrowed in thought, his mind racing with implications. "It sounds like they're up to something," he said, his voice low and tense. "If he's leaking information, we need to find out what he's telling John and who else might be involved. This could be bigger than we realize."

Chetan nodded, the gravity of the situation sinking in. "We can't let this go unchecked. If there's a mole, we need to catch them in the act. But we have to be careful. If he suspects we're onto him, he could disappear or, worse, alert John."

Fuelled by a mix of anger and determination, Aryan proposed a plan. They would survey the assistant discreetly, observing his interactions with John. If he was indeed sharing confidential information, they needed to gather evidence to confront him—and protect Chetan's family from further danger.

The next day, Aryan set up a surveillance operation. He positioned security cameras discreetly around the area where the assistant usually met John, ensuring they captured every moment. As they reviewed the footage, Aryan felt a knot tightening in his stomach. Sure enough, there it was: the assistant meeting John, their body language casual yet conspiratorial, as they exchanged whispers over steaming cups.

With each passing day, the evidence mounted. The assistant was seen slipping pieces of paper to John, and Aryan's fears were confirmed. He was the traitor, leaking information about Chetan's movements, security arrangements, and even plans for the warehouse.

Realizing the gravity of the situation, Aryan and Chetan devised a meticulous plan to confront the assistant. They needed to catch him red-handed, but the stakes were higher than just exposing a traitor. Chetan's family was in jeopardy, and if the assistant felt cornered, he could lash out in a way that would endanger them all. The balance between confrontation and caution hung precariously in the air.

Finally, the day arrived. Aryan and Chetan gathered their trusted security personnel, a tight-knit group who understood the stakes involved. They prepared to intercept the assistant as he left the office for yet another clandestine meeting. Tension clung to the atmosphere like humidity before a storm, and Aryan could feel the weight of responsibility pressing down on his shoulders, every heartbeat echoing the urgency of their mission.

As they approached the designated spot, Aryan signalled to the guards to remain hidden but ready to act at a moment's notice. He could feel his pulse quickening, adrenaline surging through him as they waited in the shadows. The minutes felt like hours, and every sound seemed amplified—the rustle of leaves, the distant hum of traffic, even the faintest whispers of the wind.

When the assistant finally arrived, Aryan stepped into view, his expression resolute and unwavering. “We need to talk,” he said, his voice low but commanding, cutting through the tension like a knife.

Caught off guard, the assistant's eyes widened, surprise morphing into a flicker of anxiety. “What are you talking about?” he stammered, attempting to mask his panic with bravado.

"You know exactly what I'm talking about," Aryan pressed, taking a step closer, his posture unyielding. "You've been feeding information to John, and we have the evidence to prove it." The truth hung in the air, thick with accusation and the promise of confrontation.

The assistant's expression shifted from shock to defiance, a hint of anger flashing in his eyes. "You have no idea what you're talking about! I'm loyal to this company!"

"Loyalty?" Aryan's voice rose slightly, fuelled by a mix of disappointment and anger. "You've betrayed us, and you're putting Chetan's family at risk. You think John is your ally? He'll use you and then throw you aside when it suits him."

Aryan's anger surged as he stepped forward, his fists clenched and a fierce determination in his eyes. "You've betrayed us, and you think you can just walk away?" He slapped the assistant across the face, the sound echoing in the quiet street. The assistant stumbled, shock etched on his features, but Aryan was ready to unleash his fury again.

However, Chetan swiftly intervened, stepping between them with a firm hand raised. "Enough, Aryan!" he commanded, his voice steady but authoritative. "We can't stoop to his level. He's already shown his true colours."

Aryan's eyes blazed with frustration, but he paused, realizing that Chetan was right. In the heat of the moment, he took a deep breath, forcing himself to step back.

Chetan turned to the assistant; his expression icy. "You're terminated. Effective immediately. Gather your things and leave the company. And if I see you anywhere near me or my family again, I won't hesitate to take action."

The assistant, still reeling from the slap and the sudden shift in power, nodded dumbly. Fear flickered across his face as he realized the gravity of his situation. "I didn't mean—"

"Save it," Aryan snapped, his voice low and menacing. "You had your chance. Now you'll face the consequences of your actions."

With that, the assistant quickly backed away, scrambling to gather his belongings. Aryan and Chetan watched him go, relieved to be rid of the last piece in the puzzle of betrayal.

As weeks turned into months, Aryan's commitment to strengthening Chetan's organization bore fruit, blossoming into a robust foundation for his new life. He tackled every issue that arose with fierce determination, his hands calloused from hard work and late nights. Each challenge was a mountain he was eager to climb, proving his worth time and again.

Whether it was negotiating with suppliers, his voice steady and authoritative, or mediating disputes among workers, his calm demeanour diffusing tensions, Aryan thrived in this new role. He was a man reborn, channelling the focus and discipline he had honed in the shadows of his past into every task at hand.

Chetan, seeing Aryan's potential, took him under his wing. He recognized not just a skilled operations head, but a leader in the making. During their late-night meetings, Chetan would share his insights, guiding Aryan through the complexities of corporate strategy. He emphasized the importance of communication, showing Aryan how to convey ideas with clarity and confidence.

"Aryan," Chetan would say, "it's not just about being right; it's about how you present your case. You have the vision, but you need to make people believe in it as much as you do."

Together, they practiced speeches and presentations. Chetan would play the role of a tough audience, throwing challenging questions Aryan's way. At first, Aryan stumbled, grappling with the nuances of public speaking. But with each session, he grew more comfortable, learning to harness his passion and articulate it effectively.

One day, during a company-wide meeting, Aryan was tasked with presenting a new initiative aimed at improving worker conditions. The room was packed with employees, some sceptical, others eager to listen. As Aryan took the stage, he felt a surge of nerves, but he recalled Chetan's advice. He took a deep breath and began.

"Thank you all for being here today. I want to start by acknowledging the hard work each of you puts in every day. It's your dedication that drives this company forward."

He spoke about the initiative not just as a policy change, but as a testament to their shared values. His voice grew stronger, more assured. "I believe that when we invest in our people, we invest in our future. Together, we can create an environment where everyone thrives."

The response was overwhelmingly positive. As he stepped down, Aryan felt a wave of relief and accomplishment wash over him. Chetan's proud nod from across the room was the affirmation he needed.

Outside of meetings, Chetan encouraged Aryan to interact more with staff at all levels. "You need to connect with them, Aryan. Show them that under your suave exterior lies a grounded and kind person. They need to see the man who cares. You're a great boss, but you need to sharpen your leadership skills. "

As Aryan settled into his role as Managing Director, which was a new promotion given to him on Chetan's insistence, a remarkable transformation began to unfold within the company. The workers and labourers, who had once viewed him with scepticism, now regarded him with reverence. It wasn't just admiration; it was as if they were worshipping him, seeing in him a leader who genuinely understood their struggles.

During lunch breaks, Aryan made it a point to remove his suit jacket and roll up his sleeves, embracing the informal atmosphere. He would often join the labourers in the cafeteria, sitting at their tables, sharing meals, and exchanging stories. With an arm casually draped around their shoulders, he would pass them bottles of water, laughing and engaging in light-hearted banter.

"Come on, Aryan sir!" one labourer would chide with a grin, "You're the boss! You can't keep getting your clothes stained sitting with us!"

But Aryan would just chuckle, waving off their concerns. "What's a little dirt when I'm surrounded by the best crew in the business?" he'd reply, his sincerity shining through.

The workers had come to appreciate this authenticity. The same labourers who had once protested against Chetan's leadership now found themselves eagerly gathering around Aryan, hanging on his every word. They were no longer just employees; they felt like part of a family, and Aryan was their protector.

He made it clear that their voices mattered, regularly inviting them to share their thoughts on workplace improvements. This inclusive approach fostered loyalty. Workers who had once been hesitant now rallied behind him, refusing to act against his interests. If a decision came down from management, they didn't grumble or resist. Instead, they worked tirelessly to uphold Aryan's vision for the company.

As Aryan continued to connect with the grassroots, he also worked closely with Chetan to strategize for the future. They held regular meetings, discussing ways to enhance employee welfare and ensure everyone felt valued. Aryan's insights, grounded in his firsthand experiences with the workers, proved invaluable.

In time, word of Aryan's leadership spread beyond the company walls, and local communities began to take notice. He was seen as a champion of the working class, a man who had risen from shadows to shine a light on the path for others. He was not just the Managing Director; he was one of them.

The labourers, once wary of corporate decisions, now wore Aryan's support like a badge of honour. It wouldn't be an exaggeration to say that they were literally eating out of his hands!

CHAPTER 8
SOARING NEW HEIGHTS

As the day approached for Chetan to leave the warehouse facility and embark on his overseas assignments, a palpable mix of excitement and sorrow filled the air. The workers, aware of his impact on their lives and community, decided to give him a farewell unlike any other.

They gathered in the main office, their faces a mix of gratitude and emotion. When Chetan stepped out, he was met with a wave of cheers, and before he could comprehend what was happening, they swept him up, lifting him onto their shoulders. Their laughter mingled with shouts of appreciation as they paraded him down the hallway, past machinery that now hummed with renewed purpose, a testament to his leadership.

As they reached the parking lot, however, the excitement was interrupted. Chetan's car refused to start, sputtering and dying with a stubbornness that seemed almost deliberate. A collective sigh of disappointment washed over the group, but the workers were undeterred. With laughter and determination, they grabbed ropes and tied them to the front of his car, flowers interwoven among the strands, transforming a simple farewell into a vibrant spectacle of affection.

As they began to pull, a worker dashed ahead, opening the bonnet of the car with a cheeky grin. "Just a little trick to make sure we could get you out of here properly!" he called back, revealing the starter cable he had discreetly removed, a playful reminder of the camaraderie that had developed between them. The group laughed, and a sense of lightness filled the air, even amidst the looming farewell.

Once outside the facility, the sight was breathtaking. Hundreds of people lined the road, standing shoulder to shoulder, hands joined in a gesture of unity and gratitude. Their faces reflected a kaleidoscope of emotions—joy, sadness, and pride—as they bid farewell to a man who had transformed their village. Chetan's heart swelled as he took in the scene. The community he had nurtured now stood before him, a living testament to the love and respect he had cultivated through his humble ways.

As his car moved slowly down the road, the flowers swayed gently in the breeze, and the workers cheered, their voices echoing with appreciation. "Thank you, Chetan sir!" they called, their voices ringing clear as if to weave a bond that would not be broken by distance. "You've changed our lives!"

Touched beyond words, Chetan felt tears welling up in his eyes. This was the love he had strived to create, the trust he had built through his actions and dedication. Each face in the crowd reminded him of the challenges they had overcome together, the hope he had instilled in their hearts.

As the car continued to move, he looked back one last time, his heart heavy yet buoyed by the knowledge that he had made a difference. The sea of joined hands, the smiles and the cheers, all echoed in his mind—a reminder that his legacy would carry on, not just in the factory's success but in the spirit of the people he had come to cherish. This farewell was not just a goodbye; it was a celebration of their journey together, a bond that would remain unbroken, no matter where he went next.

Even after Chetan moved overseas, his influence and guidance remained a constant force in Aryan's life and business endeavours. With technology bridging the distance, Chetan regularly connected with Aryan through video calls and emails, sharing insights and strategies for navigating the complexities of the Indian market. He became a mentor from afar, offering advice on everything from managing workforce dynamics to establishing crucial partnerships.

Under Chetan's watchful eye, Aryan began to develop his own business, focusing on strengthening his contacts and expanding his operations within the bustling Mumbai port. He immersed himself in the logistics of the area, understanding the intricacies of shipping routes, cargo handling, and the ever-evolving demands of the industry. With Chetan's encouragement, Aryan approached local businesses and secured contracts, quickly building a reputation as a reliable partner.

Before long, Aryan became the biggest labour contractor in his region, leveraging his understanding of worker rights and needs to foster a strong, loyal workforce. He prioritized fair wages and safe working conditions, ensuring that his employees felt valued—a lesson he had learned from Chetan's leadership style. The workers responded in kind, demonstrating their dedication and hard work, which further propelled Aryan's success.

Recognizing the potential for growth, Aryan expanded his vision and soon launched his own transport and logistics company, specializing in shipping and freight services.

When Aryan launched his transport and logistics business, he quickly discovered that success came with formidable challenges—challenges that took the form of the notorious transport mafia. This ruthless organization had long held the industry in a chokehold, and they viewed Aryan's rising influence as a direct threat to their empire.

From the moment he set up shop, Aryan was bombarded with ominous phone calls and threatening messages, each designed to instil fear and force him into submission. "You think you can just waltz in here and take over?" the voices hissed through the receiver, dripping with menace. But Aryan was not one to cower. Each threat ignited a fire within him; he was determined to fight back, no matter the cost.

Realizing that he couldn't face the mafia alone, Aryan's thoughts drifted to Rakesh. Their history was complex—a chaotic clash in prison had evolved into a grudging respect. Rakesh was a man hardened by his past, but now, freshly released and desperate for a chance at redemption, he yearned to build something meaningful. Aryan saw in him the perfect ally.

With resolve, Aryan reached out to Rakesh, offering him a position as his personal security. The moment Rakesh accepted; Aryan felt a weight lift off his shoulders. "You're not just my security," Aryan said, locking eyes with him. "You're my brother in this fight." Rakesh nodded, the weight of his own past heavy on his shoulders but determined to forge a new path. He had been trying hard to get a decent job, but just like Aryan, nobody wanted to hire an ex-criminal.

As they began their partnership, the stakes grew perilously high. Aryan was relentless, pushing forward with his business plans, but the mafia escalated their intimidation tactics. Graffiti warning him to "leave town" appeared overnight, and one evening, a car screeched to a halt outside his office. A group of thugs jumped out, brandishing hockey sticks and baseball bats, ready to send a message. Aryan's heart raced, but he stood his ground.

Rakesh was a whirlwind of action, instinctively stepping between Aryan and the approaching danger. "Get inside!" he shouted, pushing Aryan towards safety. The chaos erupted as Rakesh charged the thugs, his fists flying, turning the confrontation into a fierce brawl. Aryan watched in awe, adrenaline coursing through him as Rakesh fought valiantly, scattering the attackers with sheer grit.

As Aryan's transport business began to carve out its niche, the existing players in the industry grew increasingly agitated. The transport mafia and rival companies saw him as an intruder, a thorn in their side threatening their lucrative operations. Tensions simmered, leading to confrontations that often turned violent. Aryan and Rakesh found themselves facing not just physical threats but a deeply entrenched network of intimidation and corruption determined to maintain the status quo.

One night, after a particularly brutal skirmish with rival drivers that left Aryan's team battered but unbroken, whispers of their struggles reached Vikram, Aryan's former boss. Vikram was still a formidable mafia don, known for his no-nonsense approach and fierce loyalty to those he considered family. He had always admired Aryan's tenacity and ambition, and when he heard about the escalating threats, he knew he had to act.

Vikram decided to pay a visit to the main office of one of Aryan's fiercest rivals, a man named Raghav who had a reputation for ruthlessness. The meeting was tense, the air crackling with unspoken animosity. Raghav, a hulking figure with a permanent scowl, was surrounded by his crew, each one eyeing Vikram with suspicion.

"You've been causing a lot of trouble for a newcomer, Raghav," Vikram said, his voice steady but laced with menace. "I suggest you back off. Aryan is under my protection now, and I won't stand by while you threaten him or his business."

Raghav leaned back in his chair, feigning nonchalance. "And what's a washed-up boss like you going to do about it? This is my territory, and I don't take kindly to intruders."

Vikram's gaze hardened. "You don't understand. This isn't just about business for me; it's personal. If you continue to harass Aryan, I will make it my mission to ensure you regret it. I've built my empire on loyalty and friendship, and I don't spare my enemies."

The room fell silent as the weight of Vikram's words hung in the air. Raghav's bravado faltered for a moment; the tension palpable. "You think you can scare me?" he sneered, but there was a flicker of uncertainty in his eyes.

Vikram leaned in closer, his voice dropping to a low growl. "I've faced men like you before, and I've brought them to their knees. If you value your business and your life, you'll let Aryan operate in peace. Consider this a final warning."

With that, Vikram turned on his heel and left the room, leaving Raghav simmering in his own rage. Word of the confrontation spread like wildfire, and Raghav's crew began to murmur among themselves, a mix of fear and uncertainty creeping in.

Back at Aryan's office, the atmosphere shifted as Vikram arrived, his presence commanding respect. Aryan looked up from a stack of paperwork, relief flooding through him. "You heard about everything?"

Vikram nodded. "I've taken care of it. You're under my protection now, but you need to be smart about this. Keep your head down, build your business, and let me handle the rest. I won't let them bully you."

Aryan felt a rush of gratitude. "Thank you, Vikram. I didn't expect this kind of support."

"You're family, Aryan. Just remember, in this game, loyalty is everything. Keep only trustworthy people around you. Stand strong and don't lose sight of what you're building. We'll face them together."

With renewed confidence, Aryan focused on his business, knowing he had a powerful ally in Vikram. The balance of power began to shift, and as whispers of Vikram's intervention spread through the industry,

Aryan's enemies found themselves reconsidering their approach.

As weeks passed, Aryan's transport company began to thrive. With Rakesh by his side, they expanded operations, forging alliances and strengthening their network. The transport mafia's threats still lingered, but they were less bold now, the fear of Vikram's wrath hanging heavily over their heads.

With each successful delivery and new contract, Aryan proved that he was not just a newcomer but a force to be reckoned with. And as he built his empire, he did so with the unwavering support of his loyal team and the steadfast protection of Vikram, standing tall against any challenge that dared to come their way. But most of all, he was thankful to his friend and mentor, Chetan.

While Chetan was immersed in his overseas assignments, guiding Aryan from afar, excitement bubbled within Aryan as he prepared to unveil his first office in Mumbai. It was a significant milestone, a testament to his hard work and determination. But he wanted it to be a surprise for Chetan, a gesture of gratitude for the mentorship he had provided.

One evening, as Aryan stood in the empty office, the scent of fresh paint still lingering in the air, he dialled Chetan's number. "Hey, Chetan! I need to discuss something urgent with you. Can you make some time next week?"

Chetan's voice came through the line, filled with curiosity. "Urgent? Is everything alright? I can adjust my schedule to fly back if needed."

Aryan felt a rush of anticipation. "It's nothing to worry about, but I really can't discuss it over the phone. Just know that it's important."

Chetan hesitated for a moment, then replied, "Alright, I'll arrange my return for next week. Just let me know where to meet."

As soon as he hung up, Aryan's heart raced with excitement and nerves. This was more than just an office opening; it was a culmination of his dreams and a way to honour Chetan's belief in him. He spent the days leading up to Chetan's arrival meticulously preparing for the big reveal, ensuring everything was perfect.

Aryan's excitement was palpable as he drove to the airport, anticipation coursing through him. Chetan's arrival marked a pivotal moment in his journey, and he wanted to ensure everything went perfectly. As Chetan stepped through the terminal, Aryan's heart swelled with pride. They embraced warmly, a bond forged through challenges and triumphs.

"Welcome back, Chetan! You must be tired. Let's get you home to rest," Aryan said, leading him to the car, where his entourage waited. The air was charged with energy, and Aryan couldn't help but share his vision for the future as they drove through the bustling streets of Mumbai.

The next day, Aryan's excitement reached new heights as he prepared to reveal his new office to Chetan. He gathered his staff, ensuring everything was in place for the grand unveiling. With a sense of ceremony, Aryan drove to Chetan's residence to pick him up.

"Are you ready for a surprise?" Aryan asked, his eyes sparkling with enthusiasm. Chetan smiled, curious about what Aryan had planned.

Upon arriving at the office, Aryan led Chetan toward the entrance. "Before we go in, I need you to remove your shoes," he said, motioning toward the wet cement next to the door.

Chetan raised an eyebrow, a mix of confusion and intrigue on his face. "Take off my shoes? Why?"

"It's a tradition! It's a sign of respect for the new space, and it's also part of the ceremony we're holding today," Aryan explained, trying to keep a straight face.

Still perplexed but willing to indulge his friend, Chetan removed his shoes, revealing his polished leather soles. “Alright, what’s next?” he asked.

To Chetan’s astonishment, Aryan then requested, “Now, if you could also take off your socks.”

“Seriously?” Chetan chuckled, but he complied, intrigued by Aryan’s enthusiasm. Once he stood barefoot, Aryan pointed to the wet cement. “Now, please step in.”

Chetan hesitated, looking down at the soft, wet surface that promised to leave an imprint of his feet. “You’re kidding, right?”

“Nope! It’s tradition,” Aryan insisted. With a dramatic flair, Chetan stepped into the cement, feeling the cool substance squish between his toes. The staff watched, amused and engaged, as Aryan’s plan unfolded.

Then, to Chetan’s utter disbelief, Aryan’s team rushed forward with buckets of water, kneeling to wash Chetan’s feet. “This is definitely a first for me,” Chetan admitted, shaking his head in disbelief but unable to suppress a smile.

Once the ritual was complete, Aryan handed Chetan his footwear. “Now you can officially enter your new office,” he declared with a smile.

The reason behind Aryan's quirky ritual was deeply symbolic and heartfelt. He wanted to preserve Chetan’s footprints as a lasting tribute to the unwavering love and support that had shaped him into the person he was today. Aryan believed that every ounce of his success was rooted in Chetan's guidance, and he felt an overwhelming sense of gratitude. To him, Chetan was not just a mentor; he was a lifeline, the cornerstone of his journey.

Until that moment, the office had remained untouched, an empty canvas waiting for its purpose to be realized. Aryan was determined that Chetan would be the first to step through those doors, the one to inaugurate the space that symbolized Chetan’s mentoring and Aryan's achievements.

After the inauguration, Chetan returned home, a whirlwind of emotions swirling within him. The day had been a milestone for Aryan, and Chetan was deeply happy for him, yet it was tinged with longing for his family. He had planned a few activities to keep himself occupied, but nothing could fill the void of their absence.

As he settled into the familiar comforts of home, he picked up his phone, eager to hear the voices of his loved ones. When his wife answered, warmth flooded his heart. "Hey, love," he said, his voice laced with affection. "Today was incredible. Aryan has really outdone himself with the new office."

His wife's soft laughter rang through the line, and Chetan could almost picture her smile. "I'm so proud of you, Chetan. You've really guided him well. Aryan deserves every bit of this success."

He then turned to his sons, who were likely huddled together nearby, their excitement palpable. "Boys! Guess what? I'm in Mumbai, and Uncle Aryan just opened a new office!"

"Wow, Dad!" their voices chimed in unison, filled with enthusiasm. "Can we come visit? We want to see it!"

Chetan's heart swelled. "Of course! But tonight, I have a function that Aryan organized to celebrate. It's a bit of a big deal. I'll tell you all about it later."

The boys grumbled playfully, "Can't you skip it, Dad? We want you home!"

"I promise I'll make it up to you," he assured them, picturing their growing faces and the way they looked up to him. "You all continue to make me proud. Stay disciplined, and I'll be back before you know it."

In the evening, anticipation filled the air as Aryan arranged for his favourite car to pick up Chetan. The sleek vehicle glided through the streets of Mumbai, its polished exterior reflecting the city lights, mirroring the excitement bubbling within Chetan.

Upon arriving at the venue, Chetan was taken aback by the grand spectacle awaiting him. As he stepped out of the car, he was greeted with a vibrant fanfare. Musicians stood at the entrance, their drums pounding a rhythmic welcome and trumpets blasting jubilantly, creating an atmosphere charged with celebration. The joyful sound echoed through the evening, drawing smiles from onlookers and guests alike.

Aryan emerged from the throng, his face alight with genuine warmth. He rushed forward, arms wide open, and enveloped Chetan in a brotherly hug that spoke volumes of their friendship. "Welcome Chetan! Thanks for everything you've done for me. You're the guest of honour today," he beamed, his eyes sparkling with pride.

As the band played on, Aryan escorted Chetan towards the hall, treating him like royalty. The crowd erupted into applause, and Chetan felt a wave of emotion wash over him.

While the crowd clapped and cheered, a sense of dread prickled at the back of Aryan's mind. Years spent navigating treacherous waters had sharpened his instincts, and tonight, those instincts were screaming that something was very wrong. Scanning the joyous faces around him, Aryan's gaze fell upon a distant rooftop, where he spotted a glint of metal—a rifle barrel aimed directly at Chetan.

Panic surged through him like a wildfire. Without a second thought, Aryan lunged forward, shoving Chetan aside just as the gun fired. The sharp crack of the shot shattered the celebratory atmosphere, and the bullet grazed Chetan's side, eliciting gasps of shock from the crowd.

In an instant, chaos erupted. People screamed, scattering in every direction as the festive music faltered and was drowned out by the sound of panic. Aryan's heart raced as he quickly assessed the situation, his mind focused solely on getting Chetan to safety. Blood trickled from Chetan's wound, and Aryan felt a rush of adrenaline as he grabbed his friend, guiding him through the sea of frightened guests.

"Stay close!" Aryan shouted, urgency lacing his voice as he led Chetan toward his car, the world around them blurring into a haze of fear and confusion. He could feel the weight of the moment pressing down on him—this was supposed to be a night of celebration, not survival.

As they reached the vehicle, Aryan quickly flung open the door, helping Chetan into the seat. "Hold on!" he urged, trying to keep his voice steady despite the chaos still echoing behind them. The car roared to life, and Aryan sped away from the scene, his mind racing with thoughts of danger and uncertainty.

With sirens wailing in the distance, he pushed the accelerator, weaving through the streets. Chetan leaned back, pale and breathing heavily, and Aryan glanced over, determination burning in his chest. This attack wasn't just an isolated incident; it was a warning, and he would not let it go unanswered.

Chetan was bleeding profusely, his pallor a stark contrast to the chaos of the emergency room. As the doctors worked swiftly, their voices a blur of urgency and technical jargon, Aryan paced the waiting area, his heart pounding with anxiety.

Minutes felt like hours as the medical team assessed Chetan's injuries. Finally, a doctor emerged, wiping sweat from his brow. “He’s stable,” the doctor assured Aryan, but his expression remained serious. “He’s lucky—the bullet grazed him. If it had hit just a few inches lower, we would be dealing with a far graver situation.”

Relief washed over Aryan, though it was quickly overshadowed by the anger simmering within him. Chetan’s life had been endangered during what should have been a celebration. How had this happened? Who would dare attack him in such a public setting?

When Chetan was finally wheeled into a recovery room, Aryan rushed to his side. Chetan lay there, pale but conscious, a faint smile breaking through his pain. “You saved my life, Aryan,” he said, his voice strained but filled with gratitude.

“I’d do it again in a heartbeat,” Aryan replied, gripping Chetan’s hand tightly. “We need to figure out who did this and why.”

The police launched a full-scale inquiry into the incident, working around the clock to gather evidence and piece together the events leading up to the assassination attempt. The media, hungry for a story, seized on the chaos, creating a sensational narrative of danger lurking in the vibrant streets of Mumbai. Headlines blared about how citizens were no longer safe in their own city, turning public opinion against the rising tide of violence.

As the investigation unfolded, a grim picture emerged. Police reports indicated that the assassination attempt on Chetan was a calculated move by the transport mafia, enraged by Aryan's success in the industry. They had been watching Aryan's rapid ascent, recognizing that Chetan was the mastermind and pillar of support behind it all. By eliminating Chetan, they hoped to destabilize Aryan's business and remove a significant rival from the landscape.

The mafia knew they couldn't directly attack Aryan; that would invite the wrath of Vikram, the feared underworld don who had become a protector of sorts for Aryan. Vikram's influence was not something they wanted to tangle with. Instead, they opted for a more insidious strategy—targeting Chetan, believing that without him, Aryan would falter.

As the police conducted their interviews and gathered intelligence, Aryan remained a man on a mission. He felt the weight of Chetan's survival on his shoulders. Every detail of the attack replayed in his mind, fuelling his determination to seek revenge. He was not just fighting for his own success; he was fighting for the safety of a brother who had been there through thick and thin.

The atmosphere in the city grew tense. Rumours swirled about potential retaliation, and Aryan found himself caught in a web of fear and anger. He held a meeting with his security team, going over every possible threat and contingency. It was clear that the transport mafia would not back down easily.

As he strategized, Aryan's phone buzzed with a message from Vikram. "I've heard about the attempt on Chetan's life. We'll handle this. Just keep him safe. I have my own ways of dealing with snakes."

Aryan's fury boiled over as he paced Chetan's living room, his fists clenched in a mix of anger and helplessness. "I swear, Chetan, I will make them pay for what they did to you! They won't get away with this!"

Chetan, seated on the couch with a bandage wrapped around his shoulder, managed a calm smile. "Aryan, listen to me. This isn't the way. You have a future to focus on. Your business needs you now more than ever. You have your wife and your two wonderful sons waiting for you. They need a father who leads by example, not one who seeks revenge."

Aryan paused, the fire in his eyes flickering as Chetan's words sank in. "But they attacked you, Chetan! You're my brother. I can't just sit back while they roam free!"

Chetan reached out, placing a steady hand on Aryan's shoulder. "The law will take care of this. Trust in that. Your strength lies in your ability to rise above the chaos, to build something lasting and meaningful. Focus on that. It's what I want for you."

Reluctantly, Aryan nodded, the tension in his shoulders easing slightly. He knew Chetan was right; they had worked very hard together, and he couldn't let anger derail all their hard work.

Days later, the police made swift progress. After thorough investigations and numerous tips from informants, they managed to apprehend the individuals responsible for the attack. As the news broke, a sense of relief washed over Aryan. Those who had sought to destroy his mentor were now behind bars, facing the consequences of their actions. Aryan still wished that he could be the one who gets to punish them.

CHAPTER 9
THE VICTORY

After recovering from the assassination attempt, Chetan returned overseas, reuniting with his family and diving back into his work with renewed vigour. Known for his adventurous spirit and unwavering determination, he set his sights on a new challenge: a far-off African country where basic facilities were severely lacking.

Chetan saw potential where others saw obstacles. He envisioned a bustling port that could transform the local economy, providing jobs and essential services to the community while simultaneously expanding his organization's global footprint. With a heart full of purpose, he presented his ambitious plan to his superiors, highlighting the long-term benefits of investing in such an underdeveloped area.

"Imagine a port that not only facilitates trade but also empowers the local population," he urged, his eyes sparkling with conviction. "We can be the catalyst for change!"

His passion was contagious, and after much deliberation, the board finally leaned in, their scepticism slowly melting away.

"Chetan, you really believe this project can change lives?" Mr. Kapoor asked, his brow furrowing as he considered Chetan's proposal.

"Absolutely," Chetan replied, his voice steady and filled with conviction. "This isn't just about profit margins; it's about creating sustainable jobs and uplifting communities. We have a unique opportunity to be more than just a business."

The room buzzed with murmurs, and Chetan could sense the shifting dynamics.

"But what about the risks?" Ms. Jenny chimed in, her arms crossed, scepticism etched on her face. "What if it doesn't deliver the expected returns?"

Chetan leaned forward; his eyes locked onto hers. "Every great endeavour carries risks. But think of the potential! We can create a legacy that goes beyond our bottom line. This is our chance to impact lives positively. And as far as returns are concerned, do you doubt my abilities?"

Silence hung in the air as he continued, "I know I've faced challenges in my journey, but that's what fuels my determination. This project represents hope, not just for us but for countless families who depend on us. I know we don't work for charity. Don't worry about the bottom-line profits. I will deliver results."

The tension in the room thickened, and Chetan felt a surge of urgency. "Imagine being part of something that lifts people from despair. We owe it to those who believe in us."

After a moment that felt like an eternity, Mr. Kapoor finally nodded, his expression softening. "Alright, Chetan. If we're going to take this leap, we do it together. You have never let this company down in the past, and I have complete faith you will excel in the future as well. Let's back your vision."

Supportive murmurs rippled through the boardroom, and Chetan's heart swelled with hope.

With the green light secured, Chetan travelled to the African country, immersing himself in the culture and forging connections with local leaders. He faced numerous challenges—bureaucratic red tape, resource shortages, and even scepticism from the community. But Chetan's unwavering belief in his mission fuelled his persistence. He spent long days on-site, working alongside local labourers, listening to their concerns, and involving them in the decision-making process.

Slowly but surely, the port began to take shape. Chetan's tireless efforts and innovative approaches attracted attention from neighbouring countries, and the project started gaining international recognition. Soon, what began as a single port evolved into a network of facilities across various countries, each one tailored to meet local needs and enhance trade routes.

As the ports flourished, Chetan's company soared to new heights. With each successful project, he remained grounded, always reminding his team that their success was intertwined ,with the well-being of the communities they served. For Chetan, this was more than just business; it was a legacy of hope and empowerment that he was determined to build, one port at a time.

Chetan's career was defined by a series of challenging assignments that tested his resolve and tenacity. Wherever there was a crisis that others avoided, the board of directors turned to him, confident in his ability to navigate the storm. He had earned a reputation as a no-nonsense leader—a man who faced adversity head-on and emerged victorious.

From war-torn regions to remote villages grappling with natural disasters, Chetan tackled each hardship with unwavering determination. In one instance, he was sent to a conflict zone where tensions ran high and fear was palpable. While others hesitated, he stepped onto the ground, engaging with local leaders and communities. His calm demeanour and willingness to listen fostered trust, transforming hostile environments into collaborative spaces.

During another assignment, Chetan found himself in an area ravaged by a devastating earthquake. The devastation was terrible; buildings lay in ruins, and the air was thick with dust. As the company's representative, he felt a profound sense of responsibility. This was not just a job; it was a calling.

"Gather everyone! We need to set up a command centre!" Chetan shouted, his voice rising above the chaos. He watched as volunteers rushed to his side; eyes filled with determination.

"Where do we start?" asked Kagiso, a local volunteer, his brow furrowed with concern.

"First, we assess the damage and prioritize our efforts. We need to provide immediate aid—food, water, medical supplies. Let's coordinate with the local officials," Chetan replied, already mapping out a plan in his mind.

As they moved through the debris-strewn streets, Chetan's heart ached for the families affected. He stopped to speak with a distraught mother clutching her child, her eyes wide with fear. "We're here to help you," he assured her, kneeling to meet her gaze. "We will get you the resources you need."

He worked tirelessly alongside volunteers and local officials, embodying the belief that true leadership means rolling up your sleeves and working shoulder to shoulder with those in need. Chetan helped distribute supplies, his hands dirty but his spirit unyielded.

"Over here! We've set up a distribution point!" he called out, waving his arms to gather people. As families began to line up, Chetan felt a wave of purpose wash over him. Each grateful smile strengthened his resolve.

"Thank you for being here," one elderly man said, tears in his eyes. "You're giving us hope. I'm sure God has sent you to save us."

Chetan smiled back, the warmth of their gratitude igniting a fire within him. “Don’t thank me, sir. This is just the beginning. We’ll rebuild your lives together.”

As the sun began to set, painting the sky in hues of orange and pink, Chetan took a moment to reflect on the day's work. He could see the hope returning to the eyes of the community, and in that moment, he realized that this was why he fought so hard—to make a difference when it mattered most.

Chetan's bosses were thoroughly impressed when they learned of the extensive efforts, he had taken to help the locals through such a tough time. News of his leadership during the earthquake relief spread quickly, transforming the company’s image in the community. Where there had once been scepticism, there was now admiration and gratitude.

“Chetan, the reports are incredible!” his manager, Mr. Kapoor, exclaimed during a company-wide meeting. “Your dedication has not only helped the victims but has also brought about a spirit of unity among our workers. The locals now see us as friends, not just a corporation.”

As the applause rang out, Chetan felt a swell of pride. The workers, motivated by his example, were giving their all, pouring their hearts into every task. Productivity had soared, and the atmosphere in the office was electric with optimism.

"Along with public sentiment, our productivity has improved tremendously," Mr. Kapoor continued, his eyes gleaming with excitement. "The profits this year are unexpectedly high—something we could only dream of!"

Chetan's heart raced as his efforts were recognized. The hard work, the long hours spent coordinating relief, and the sleepless nights were finally paying off.

"To celebrate this success," Mr. Kapoor announced, "we're offering Chetan a hefty bonus. You've not only set a new standard for our company, but you've also shown what true leadership looks like. Congratulations!"

The room erupted into cheers, and Chetan felt a mix of humility and elation wash over him. He hadn't done it for recognition, but the acknowledgment was a powerful validation of his beliefs.

"Thank you," Chetan said, his voice steady despite the whirlwind of emotions. "This isn't just my success—it's a testament to the hard work of everyone here. This success belongs to everybody."

As the applause faded, he caught a glimpse of his colleagues, their faces beaming with pride and inspiration.

Chetan's no-nonsense approach earned him both respect and admiration. He navigated the corporate landscape with a blend of tenacity and integrity that set him apart. When faced with corruption or inefficiency, he didn't hesitate to confront the issues head-on.

"Listen, we can't turn a blind eye to this," he stated firmly during a heated meeting, his voice steady as he faced a room full of sceptical colleagues. "If we allow this to continue, we're not just jeopardizing our reputation; we're betraying the trust of those we serve."

His colleagues exchanged uneasy glances, some shifting in their seats. "Chetan, we have to consider the consequences," one of them warned. "This isn't just about us. It could impact our bottom line."

"Exactly," Chetan countered, his passion igniting the room. "It's about our bottom line in the long run! Cutting corners today will come back to haunt us tomorrow. We have to advocate for transparency and accountability, even if it's uncomfortable."

Though his unwavering commitment often set him at odds with complacent colleagues, he remained resolute. Chetan understood that real leadership sometimes meant standing alone, but he took pride in his principles.

On another occasion, when a particularly corrupt contract was under discussion, he gathered his courage and confronted his superiors. “We can’t go through with this deal,” he insisted, his heart racing. “It’s unethical and it undermines everything we’ve worked for.”

“Chetan, you need to think strategically,” his boss replied dismissively. “This could secure our position in the market.”

“But at what cost?” Chetan shot back, his voice rising with conviction. “If we sacrifice our integrity for profit, we’ll lose everything that truly matters in the long run. Our reputation is our most valuable asset.”

His commitment to doing what was right often placed him at odds with the more complacent elements within the company, but he was unfazed. Chetan believed that integrity would always outshine short-term gains. With every challenge he faced, his resolve only deepened, and he became a beacon of inspiration for those who valued honesty over convenience.

While Chetan was tirelessly working around the world, Aryan was establishing his own empire back in Mumbai. He had transformed his initial venture into a thriving enterprise, expanding rapidly with a determination that seemed unstoppable. His business was no longer just local; he had set up several agencies across the country, each one more successful than the last.

Aryan's vision was bold, and his ambition knew no bounds. With a sharp mind and relentless drive, he turned challenges into opportunities, often surprising even himself with what he could achieve. The bustling streets of Mumbai became a backdrop to his success, as he navigated the competitive landscape with the finesse of a seasoned entrepreneur.

Emboldened by his achievements and Chetan's steadfast support, Aryan decided to venture into international waters. The thrill of exploring new markets sent adrenaline coursing through his veins. He meticulously researched opportunities in four different countries, immersing himself in diverse cultures and economic landscapes.

Each new venture felt like a grand adventure, filled with uncertainty and promise. He attended international trade fairs, connected with local entrepreneurs, and absorbed the nuances of each market.

In Singapore, he forged partnerships that opened doors to the tech industry; in Dubai, he tapped into the luxury goods sector; in Brazil, he explored eco-friendly products; and in South Africa, he sought to empower local artisans.

With each new venture, Aryan demonstrated an uncanny ability to adapt and thrive. He wasn't just building a business; he was crafting a legacy. His relentless pursuit of excellence attracted attention, and soon he was hosting meetings with influential investors and industry leaders. The thrill of success fuelled his ambition further, and he became known as a rising star in the business world.

Throughout this whirlwind of growth, Aryan relied heavily on Chetan's wisdom. Late-night phone calls became a ritual, their conversations often stretching into the early hours of the morning. "Chetan," Aryan would say, his voice a mix of excitement and trepidation, "I'm looking at this new market in Brazil. The potential is huge, but the competition is fierce. What do you think?"

Chetan's voice would come through the line, steady and reassuring. "Take the leap, Aryan. Do your homework, of course, but don't shy away from calculated risks. Remember, the biggest rewards often come from the boldest moves. Just ensure you have a solid backup plan."

Those words became Aryan's mantra. Chetan's insights, drawn from his vast experience in international projects and crisis management, provided Aryan with the confidence he needed to take calculated risks. Each piece of advice felt like a lifeline, helping him navigate the turbulent waters of entrepreneurship.

Despite the physical distance between them, they were always close. Aryan often found inspiration in Chetan's adventurous spirit. "I just wrapped up a project in the aftermath of that earthquake," Chetan shared during one call. "The resilience of the people there was incredible. It reminded me that every challenge is an opportunity to make a real impact."

Motivated by Chetan's relentless drive to make a difference, Aryan pushed the boundaries of his own aspirations. He started viewing every setback as a chance to grow, his perspective shifting toward the positive. Whenever Aryan faced challenges—be it logistical hurdles or competitive threats—Chetan was just a phone call away, ready with solutions and encouragement.

"Remember when we tackled that project in college together?" Chetan would often remind him.

"You were always the one who found a way to turn obstacles into stepping stones. You've got this."

Their friendship was a solid foundation amidst the chaos of Aryan's rapidly changing life. But the pressure was mounting. One night, as Aryan stared at the wall of his office, a thousand thoughts racing through his mind, he picked up the phone once again. "Chetan, I'm feeling the weight of this expansion. What if I fail?"

There was a pause, and then Chetan's voice came through, calm and steady. "Failure is just a stepping stone, Aryan. What matters is how you rise from it. You're not alone in this. Keep your vision clear, and don't forget the people who believe in you—especially Vani and those two boys."

In that moment, Aryan felt a renewed sense of purpose. The warmth of Chetan's unwavering support fuelled his determination. He knew he could face the challenges ahead, fortified by the knowledge that he wasn't just building a business; he was crafting a legacy for his family.

After decades of globe-trotting and relentless hard work, Chetan felt a profound shift within himself. It was time to hang up his boots and embark on a new journey—one that prioritized his own passions and desires. He had dedicated much of his life to building ports for companies across the globe, rescuing businesses from the brink of financial collapse, and serving as a special advisor to the government on infrastructure development. His contributions had not only transformed landscapes but had also left a lasting impact on countless communities.

As he reflected on his illustrious career, Chetan realized that he had achieved everything he had once dreamed of. Yet, amid the accolades and successes, he had also felt tethered to his suitcase, living out of hotel rooms and conference halls. The constant travel had taken a toll on him; he longed for the comfort of home, for the simple pleasures of life that he had often overlooked in the pursuit of ambition.

With a sense of clarity, Chetan decided it was time to step back from the fast-paced corporate world and embrace a life that transcended mere transactions. He envisioned a future where he could give back to the community, mentor the next generation of leaders, and perhaps even write about his experiences to inspire others.

Chetan returned to India, filled with a sense of purpose and a desire to give back to the world that had shaped him. With his wealth of experience and a deep understanding of global markets, he transitioned into freelance consulting. His reputation as a no-nonsense expert preceded him, and businesses eager for guidance sought his expertise.

He began by working with startups and established companies alike, helping them navigate the complexities of offshore operations. Chetan immersed himself in each project, analysing their needs and tailoring strategies that would not only stabilize their financial footing but also promote sustainable growth. His insights into market dynamics and operational efficiencies became invaluable as he advised on everything from supply chain logistics to regulatory compliance.

Chetan's approach was hands-on. He would often visit companies in person, immersing himself in their culture and operations. This not only allowed him to gain a comprehensive understanding of their challenges but also built strong relationships with his clients. He believed in the power of collaboration, and he made it a point to empower the teams he worked with, fostering a sense of ownership and accountability.

One of Chetan's first significant projects involved a mid-sized manufacturing company that was grappling with crippling inefficiencies in its international logistics. The atmosphere in the office was tense; employees were overworked, and management was anxious about falling behind competitors. Chetan arrived on the scene with a clear purpose and an unwavering determination to turn things around.

He conducted a thorough assessment, meticulously analysing every aspect of their supply chain. Chetan spent long hours poring over data, observing operations on the ground, and engaging with employees at all levels. "We need to identify the bottlenecks that are holding you back," he told the anxious CEO during their initial meeting. "This isn't just about reducing costs; it's about reimagining how you do business."

His approach was hands-on and collaborative. Chetan organized brainstorming sessions that included everyone from warehouse staff to upper management. He believed in the power of collective insight and encouraged employees to voice their concerns and suggestions. "You're the backbone of this company," he reminded them. "Your experiences matter."

As he dissected their logistics process, Chetan discovered several critical issues: outdated software, inefficient routing, and poor communication among departments. Armed with this knowledge, he began to implement strategic negotiations with suppliers and partners, leveraging his connections to secure better rates and terms. He proposed innovative solutions like integrating a new inventory management system that utilized real-time data, drastically improving order accuracy and turnaround times.

The results were nothing short of transformative. Within months, the company experienced a remarkable turnaround. Costs were slashed, efficiency soared, and the once-unstable manufacturing operation began to stabilize. Employees who had once felt overwhelmed now wore smiles of relief and optimism. The CEO could hardly contain his excitement as he reported to Chetan, "We're finally in a position to expand our reach into new markets! This is incredible!"

Chetan's heart swelled with pride. He had not only salvaged a company but had also ignited a newfound sense of purpose among its employees. His reputation for driving change quickly spread, and soon, other businesses began to seek him out for his expertise.

As Chetan moved on to his next project, he couldn't shake the satisfaction he felt from this success. He was reminded of the power of collaboration and the impact of listening to those on the front lines. But even amidst these triumphs, he remained vigilant, aware that challenges awaited him at every turn.

The business world was ruthless, and Chetan knew he had to stay one step ahead—not just for himself but for everyone relying on him to lead the way. Each project was not just a job; it was a chance to make a difference, to create change that rippled beyond the balance sheet. With every success, Chetan's resolve grew stronger, fuelling his passion to tackle even more ambitious projects.

Chetan found immense fulfilment in mentoring young entrepreneurs, believing that the next generation held the keys to a brighter future. He initiated workshops and seminars, converting conference rooms into vibrant spaces of learning and inspiration. Each session began with a compelling story from his own journey. He spoke about the challenges he had faced, the failures that had shaped him, and the triumphs that had followed.

"Success isn't just about profits," he would say, his voice resonating with passion. "It's about resilience, integrity, and the impact you make on others. You have the power to change the world, but it must start with your values."

His workshops were more than just lectures; they were interactive experiences. Chetan encouraged participants to share their own stories, fostering an environment where vulnerability and ambition coexisted. He'd often pose questions that forced them to reflect deeply: "What drives you? What do you want to be remembered for?"

One memorable session took place at a local community centre, where a diverse group of budding entrepreneurs gathered. Among them was Maya, a single mother determined to start her own bakery. Chetan noticed her hesitation during a brainstorming exercise, so he pulled her aside. "What's holding you back?" he asked gently.

"I just don't think I have what it takes," she confessed, her voice trembling.

Chetan leaned in; his eyes filled with understanding. "I once felt the same way. But let me tell you, it's the struggle that makes you stronger. Embrace your journey, learn from it, and use it to fuel your passion. Your story will resonate with your customers. They'll see your heart in every pastry."

Inspired by Chetan's encouragement, Maya took the leap. Over the following months, she blossomed from a hesitant dreamer into a confident entrepreneur, her bakery becoming a beloved local spot. Chetan kept in touch, celebrating her successes and offering guidance through challenges. Today, Maya owns a chain of bakeries, and is one of the most respected names in her business.

The ripple effects of Chetan's mentorship extended far beyond individual successes. His emphasis on ethics and resilience began to create a culture among his mentees—a group of entrepreneurs who prioritized integrity over shortcuts. They supported one another, sharing resources and advice, and challenging each other to maintain their values even when tempted by easier paths.

As word spread about Chetan's workshops, attendance grew, and so did his influence. Young entrepreneurs would approach him after sessions, eager to glean insights from his experiences. "You make it feel possible," one attendee remarked after a particularly inspiring seminar. "Thank you for showing us that dreams can be pursued ethically."

With each encounter, Chetan realized that mentoring was not just about imparting knowledge; it was about igniting a spark of possibility in others. He found joy in watching his mentees grow, thrive, and carve out their own paths, each one carrying forward the lessons he had instilled in them.

As he continued to consult for various businesses, Chetan felt a sense of satisfaction that came from watching others succeed. He was no longer just building ports and financial strategies; he was building futures by nurturing talent, instilling confidence, and encouraging a spirit of innovation.

Through his consulting work, Chetan not only established a new chapter in his life but also solidified his legacy as a mentor and guide, ensuring that his contributions would ripple through the industry for years to come.

Once, after what felt like ages, Aryan and Chetan finally found time to catch up over lunch at a swanky restaurant in Mumbai. The atmosphere buzzed with energy, but a more profound tension simmered beneath their conversation. As they sipped their drinks and savoured the exquisite dishes, Aryan leaned in, his eyes intense with purpose.

"I've been thinking about entering politics," he said, his voice steady but filled with conviction.

Chetan raised an eyebrow, taken aback. "Politics? That's quite a leap. What's driving this decision?"

Aryan sighed, recalling the scars of his past. "I've built a business empire, Chetan. I've achieved a lot in terms of wealth and success, but it feels hollow. I see the struggles of the youth, the corruption that festers in our society, and I can't just stand by anymore. I want to be a voice for them."

Chetan nodded, understanding the weight of those words. "But politics is a treacherous game. It's not just about intent; it's about navigating a web of deceit, alliances, and rivalries. Are you ready for that?"

"Absolutely," Aryan declared, his eyes igniting with determination. "I recently had a run-in with some local goons—backed by a politician who's utterly corrupt. I witnessed how those in power prey on the vulnerable, and it made my blood boil. I realized that if I want to effect real change, I can't just sit on the sidelines."

Chetan leaned forward, concern knitting his brows. "What happened? Were you hurt?"

"No, thankfully," Aryan said, brushing it off. "But it was a stark wake-up call. I watched as they bullied local vendors, extorting money with menacing grins while the politician turned a blind eye. It was like a light switch flipped in my mind. If I want to stand up for these people, I have to step into the arena myself."

Chetan's gaze intensified, the weight of Aryan's words hanging in the air. "It takes a lot of courage to go down that road. But you're right; change starts with those willing to fight for it. Just know the battle will be fierce."

"I get that," Aryan replied, his voice firm. "But I've fought my share of battles—this is just another one. I want to be the voice for those who feel powerless, to restore transparency and integrity to our society."

"Your heart is in the right place," Chetan said, a mix of admiration and caution flickering in his eyes. "But remember, the political world is merciless. They won't hesitate to target you if they feel threatened."

"I know the risks," Aryan assured him, his conviction unwavering. "But I can't stand by while people suffer. I have to try."

Chetan leaned back in his chair, studying Aryan's determined expression. "Okay," he finally said, a note of caution threading through his voice. "But be very cautious, and keep your nose clean."

Aryan nodded, fully aware of the weight behind those words. Chetan had a unique perspective; he wasn't just any friend—he was the nephew of a late political bigwig, someone who had navigated the treacherous waters of politics firsthand. Chetan knew the shadows that lurked behind the façade of power, the compromises that often-led good intentions astray.

"I know how difficult this life can be," Chetan continued, his tone serious. "Politics isn't just about making speeches and shaking hands. It's a murky world filled with temptation and betrayal. I've seen it up close, and I don't want you to fall into the same traps."

"Believe me, I'll be careful," Aryan replied, his resolve firm. "I won't let the darkness change who I am or what I stand for. I want to be a force for good, to uplift those who've been neglected."

Chetan smiled, proud of his friend's conviction. "I admire that. But just remember, it's easy to lose sight of your principles when the stakes are high. Stay grounded, and don't let the allure of power blind you."

"I promise," Aryan assured him, the weight of responsibility settling on his shoulders. "Your guidance means everything to me."

With a heavy sigh, Chetan reached across the table and placed a hand on Aryan's. "You have my blessings, my friend. Just be vigilant. Surround yourself with people who share your vision, and don't hesitate to lean on me when things get tough."

Aryan felt a swell of gratitude. "Thank you, Chetan. Your support is invaluable. I'll make you proud."

As their lunch progressed, they delved into the pros and cons of Aryan's ambitious plans. Chetan shared insights from his own experiences, emphasizing the importance of integrity and authenticity in politics. They debated, discussed strategies, and reminisced about their shared history, but the gravity of Aryan's ambition hung over the conversation, a reminder of the challenges ahead.

By the end of the meal, Aryan felt relieved, more certain than ever that he was ready to take this leap into the political arena. He had the support of his friend, and that meant the world to him.

After that pivotal discussion with Chetan, Aryan embarked on his political journey with fervour. Armed with his business acumen and a vision for change, he began reaching out to influential political figures, navigating the corridors of power with strong determination. As he approached these bigwigs, he articulated his desire to join their party, outlining his commitment to serve the community and fight corruption.

The party leaders scrutinized him intensely. They delved into every detail of his past, examining his struggles to break free from a life tainted by violence and chaos. His impressive rise in the business world caught their attention, but it was his resilience that truly stood out. They appreciated that he wasn't just a man of wealth; he was a survivor who had faced adversity head-on.

"Politics requires money, and you've got it," one member remarked, glancing at Aryan's financial statements. "But more importantly, we need strong characters who won't buckle under pressure. You've seen enough bloodshed to know how to stand your ground."

Aryan nodded, recalling the countless battles he had fought, both on the streets and in boardrooms. He was no stranger to threats, and he had powerful allies, men like Vikram, the notorious underworld don, who had his back. This gave him an edge that few could match.

After a thorough evaluation, the party's top brass decided to grant Aryan a ticket to contest the upcoming elections. They believed he could galvanize support, attract voters with his charm, and leverage his financial resources for campaign efforts. To announce this decision, they organized a grand welcome function, pulling out all the stops.

The venue was buzzing with anticipation as Aryan arrived, greeted by raucous applause and flashing cameras. The atmosphere was electric, filled with a mix of hope and scepticism. Dignitaries and supporters gathered, eager to hear Aryan's vision for change. He stepped onto the stage, heart racing, ready to make his mark in the political arena.

"Today marks the beginning of a new chapter," he declared, voice steady and powerful. "I stand before you not just as a candidate, but as someone who understands the struggles we face. Together, we will reclaim our dignity, fight corruption, and ensure that every voice is heard."

Cheers erupted from the crowd, but Aryan knew that this was just the beginning. The path ahead would be filled with challenges, but he was ready to face them head-on, armed with the belief that he could make a change in this world.

Aryan had just eight months to prepare for the elections, and he was all in. The gravity of the task ahead was enormous - an election campaign is no walk in the park, but he embraced it with the fervour of a man on a mission. His two sons were sent off to London, enrolled in prestigious schools, ensuring they could focus solely on their studies, shielded from the whirlwind of Aryan's political ambitions. It was a sacrifice, but one that he believed was necessary for their future.

Meanwhile, Aryan was busy setting up his new headquarters, a sleek office designed to reflect his newfound ambition and seriousness about his political journey. He envisioned it as a hub of activity, where ideas would flourish and strategies would take shape. A place where people could come to approach him with their problems, and he could work out solutions to help them. As the walls went up and furniture was arranged, he felt a thrill of excitement mixed with a hint of anxiety—this was uncharted territory.

Chetan, occupied with an international assignment alongside a burgeoning entrepreneur who desperately needed his expertise, regrettably couldn't be there for the office's inauguration. But Aryan made sure to honour his friend's influence and support in the most meaningful way.

Before officially opening the doors, Aryan took a moment to reserve a special room—Chetan's cabin. It was a gesture of gratitude and respect, a symbolic space that would forever remind him of the man who had been his mentor and guiding light. The walls were adorned with an elegant picture of Lord Ganesha, symbolizing wisdom and prosperity. But the centrepiece was the pedestal that housed Chetan's cemented footprints, encased in glass—a permanent tribute to the foundation upon which Aryan was building his future.

When the inauguration day arrived, Aryan stood in the centre of the new office, looking around at the team he had assembled. They were eager, bright-eyed, and ready to tackle the challenges ahead. He felt a rush of determination as he addressed them.

"This office represents not just my political journey but a commitment to the values that Chetan instilled in me," he declared, his voice steady and inspiring. "With his footprints here, we remind ourselves of the sacrifices made for our dreams and the integrity we must uphold in every decision."

As he cut the ceremonial ribbon, Aryan knew that while Chetan couldn't be there physically, his presence was felt in every corner of the office. He was stepping into a new chapter, not just for himself, but for the people he aimed to serve, and Chetan would always be a part of that journey.

Aryan threw himself into his campaign with an intensity that bordered on obsession. The next few months saw him canvassing in every corner of his constituency, from sprawling playgrounds echoing with laughter to narrow, bustling streets that whispered stories of struggle. He knocked on doors, greeted families, and listened intently to the challenges they faced, which were issues that ranged from frequent electricity cuts that left them in darkness to water shortages that plagued their daily lives.

The stark contrast between Aryan and his opponent, a polished politician hailing from an affluent family, was evident. This rival was notorious for appearing only during election campaigns, charming voters with promises that vanished as soon as he secured their votes. Aryan saw the frustration etched in the faces of the constituents, and it fuelled his resolve. He was not just another candidate; he was a neighbour, a friend who genuinely cared.

During public rallies, Aryan didn't hold back. His voice rang out, sharp and clear, as he launched a scathing war of words against his opponent. "You've been absent when it mattered most!" he declared, his passion electrifying the crowd. "Your luxurious life has shielded you from the reality we face every day! You come here to kiss babies and shake hands, but when the cameras turn off, you vanish!"

The audience erupted in applause, the resonance of his words echoing in their hearts. Aryan vowed to dedicate every ounce of his energy and resources to their upliftment if he won. "Imagine a community where children play freely without fear of darkness! A place where families can trust their government to provide basic needs! That's the future I want for us, and I won't stop until we achieve it together!"

His campaign took on a life of its own, fuelled by grassroots support that seemed to blossom overnight. Aryan hosted community meetings in local parks, transforming mundane gatherings into vibrant discussions where everyone felt heard. "This is your chance to speak up," he urged, his voice rising with conviction. "What do you want for our neighbourhood?" As hands shot up, each voice added another layer to the tapestry of his vision—a vision rooted in their hopes and struggles.

Energized by the enthusiasm around him, Aryan assembled teams of dedicated volunteers. Together, they knocked on doors, not just to solicit votes, but to forge connections. They distributed pamphlets detailing his plans, each interaction igniting a spark of community spirit. "Have you met Aryan yet?" one volunteer would say to a hesitant neighbour. "He's genuinely here to listen." Those simple words broke down barriers, inviting people into a conversation rather than a campaign pitch.

As the election date loomed closer, the atmosphere buzzed with anticipation, charged with a mix of excitement and anxiety. Aryan knew he was in a fierce battle, but his determination remained unshakeable. He wasn't just campaigning for a seat in office; he was fighting for the people who had been overlooked for too long, those who felt invisible in a system that often ignored their voices.

With every challenge he faced—be it the mudslinging from rival candidates or the logistical nightmares of organizing events—he remembered Chetan's advice: to stay true to his values and always put the community first. "This is about them, not me," he reminded himself during late-night strategy sessions, as fatigue tugged at his eyelids.

The turning point came during a heated town hall meeting. A local resident stood up, anger flashing in his eyes. "Why should we trust you, Aryan? You're just another politician, right?" The room fell silent, tension hanging in the air like a storm cloud.

Taking a deep breath, Aryan met the man's gaze, his heart pounding in his chest. "You're right to question me," he replied, his voice steady but heartfelt. "But I'm not here to make empty promises. I'm here to earn your trust, day by day, conversation by conversation. I want to work alongside you, not just for you. What can we do together to make this community better?"

The sincerity in his tone shifted the atmosphere. Murmurs of agreement rippled through the crowd, and the man's expression softened. "I just want to know that someone cares," he admitted, and Aryan could see the vulnerability behind the anger.

"Then let's start caring together," Aryan said, extending his hand as a gesture of unity. The crowd erupted in applause, and the connection solidified. It was in that moment Aryan became more than just a candidate; he was emerging as a beacon of hope.

As the days turned into a blur of rallies and phone calls, Aryan's efforts paid off. The people began to see him not just as another politician, but as a genuine leader committed to uplifting their lives. They felt his sincerity in every conversation, every promise, and his unwavering dedication to their cause. The warmth of his connection with the community grew stronger, and they rallied behind him, eager for change.

In the final stretch of the campaign, Aryan organized a massive rally, hoping to galvanize the momentum he had built. As he stood before a sea of supporters, the energy in the air was electric. "Together, we are not just a gathering, we are a force!" he declared, his voice resonating through the crowd. "Let's make history together!"

And with that powerful message, Aryan pressed on, fuelled by the passion and belief of those he had come to love. The election was not just a contest; it was a movement, and he was ready to lead them into a future that promised to be brighter than ever before.

But as Aryan's popularity soared, his rival began to panic, feeling the ground shift beneath his feet. Fearing the loss of his seat, he resorted to desperate tactics that echoed the worst of political gamesmanship. One sunny afternoon, the streets buzzed with an unsettling energy, a sharp contrast to the hopeful rallies Aryan had cultivated.

Cash and gifts began circulating like wildfire, infiltrating the neighbourhood with an insidious charm. The opposition camp set up booths adorned with flashy banners and smiling faces, handing out money like it was confetti at a parade. "Free groceries! Cash giveaways!" the signs proclaimed, enticing locals with promises of immediate rewards. The atmosphere grew thick with the scent of corruption, a sharp contrast to Aryan's vision of a community-driven future.

When Aryan learned of the blatant attempt to buy votes, his anger ignited like a wildfire. The integrity of the election was under siege, and he couldn't stand idly by. The next rally was a pivotal moment; he stepped onto the stage with fire in his eyes, fuelled by righteous indignation. "You've seen the truth for yourselves!" he declared, his voice slicing through the murmur of the crowd like a sharpened blade. "My opponent thinks he can fool you with his cash and trinkets!"

The crowd stirred; their attention drawn to his fervour. "But let me remind you: this money is not his. It should be used for the development of our locality—for better schools, roads, and healthcare! Instead, he's trying to buy your trust, to distract you from the real issues we face!"

A roar of agreement erupted from the audience, their loyalty to Aryan deepening with each word. He pressed on, his passion rising to a crescendo. "This is your future we're talking about! Do you want to be treated like pawns in a game? Or do you want someone who truly cares about your lives and is willing to fight for you?"

Every syllable resonated deeply, igniting a sense of pride and resolve among the people. They realized this wasn't just an election; it was a chance to reclaim their dignity, to stand against manipulation and deception. Hope flickered in their eyes as Aryan's voice grew stronger, more insistent.

"Stand with me!" he shouted, his arms raised high, rallying their spirits. "Let's show him that our voices cannot be bought! Together, we can create a community that thrives, not one that is held hostage by empty promises and handouts!"

The atmosphere crackled with electricity as Aryan's speech gained momentum. His words painted a vivid picture of what their future could look like—schools filled with eager children, safe streets, and a community bound by mutual respect and support.

The contrast between Aryan's authentic vision and his opponent's bribery became crystal clear, like a beacon shining through the fog of corruption. "You have the power to choose!" he continued, his voice now a powerful anthem. "Do you want to let fear dictate your decisions? Or do you want to rise up, to reclaim your voices and your futures?"

The crowd was on their feet, a wave of energy surging through them as they cheered for change. Aryan's fiery rhetoric not only called out the opposition's underhanded tactics but also inspired a movement, igniting hope and determination in every heart present.

Eventually, the day of the elections arrived, and the air was thick with anticipation. Aryan sat at home, his heart pounding, with Vani by his side, holding his hand tightly. The television screen flickered with images of polling stations and excited crowds as they waited for the results to be announced. Every second felt like an eternity.

When the results began to roll in, Aryan's breath caught in his throat. One by one, the numbers flashed across the screen, confirming what he had worked so hard for. He had won. No, he had triumphed—with a landslide victory that shattered expectations. The opposition, once a formidable force, had crumbled, their numbers dwindling to a mere whisper in the chaos of the results. The election was completely lopsided, a historic moment in the constituency. Aryan let out a roar of pure joy, a sound of triumph that reverberated through their home, echoing off the walls like a declaration of victory.

In an explosive surge of energy, he leapt up, scooping Vani into his arms, their celebration bursting forth like a long-held breath finally released. "We did it! We actually did it!" he exclaimed, spinning her around as laughter bubbled from her lips, mingling with his cries of joy. The weight of every challenge they had faced melted away in that moment, replaced by sheer exhilaration.

"Look at the numbers!" Vani said, her eyes sparkling with disbelief and pride. "You crushed it, Aryan! You showed them what true leadership looks like!"

He set her down gently, his hands still resting on her shoulders, searching her gaze for affirmation. "We did this together, Vani. Your support, your faith—it made all the difference."

His face filled the news channels, glowing with victory. Anchors praised his leadership skills, hailing him as the best new leader of the country. "The people's choice," they declared, as footage of cheering supporters filled the screen. Aryan could hardly believe it—he was no longer just a candidate; he was a symbol of hope and change. The public had spoken, and they had embraced him as their own.

Just then, his phone began to ring incessantly. Congratulations poured in from friends, family, and well-wishers. The chief of his political party called repeatedly, eager to share in the jubilation. But amidst the excitement, Aryan felt a rush of gratitude that overshadowed everything else. He needed to reach out to the one person who had believed in him from the very start.

Ignoring the flurry of notifications, Aryan dialled Chetan's number. The phone rang, and with each tone, he felt a surge of anticipation. When Chetan picked up, Aryan wasted no time. "Chetan! I did it! I won!" His voice was filled with exhilaration, the weight of his success palpable through the line.

Chetan's laughter erupted on the other end, a sound of pure joy that resonated deeply. “I knew you would! You’ve worked so hard for this, Aryan. You deserve every bit of this victory!”

“I couldn’t have done it without you,” Aryan replied, emotion thickening his voice. “Your guidance and support meant the world to me. You believed in me when I wasn’t sure I believed in myself.”

Chetan’s response was warm and reassuring. “You found the strength within you. All I did was help you see it. Now, the real work begins. This victory is just the first step.”

As they spoke, Aryan’s heart swelled with pride and gratitude. He could picture Chetan's smile, the way his eyes sparkled with encouragement. “I’ll do my best for these people,” Aryan promised, his resolve solidifying. “I’m going to make sure my people get everything they need and more.”

After the call ended, Aryan turned back to Vani, who was beaming with pride. They embraced again, knowing this was just the beginning of a journey that would challenge them both but also fill their lives with purpose.

As the celebrations continued around him, Aryan couldn't help but feel that the victory wasn't just his. It belonged to everyone who had stood by him, supported him, and believed in a brighter future. With renewed determination, he was ready to step into the role he had fought for, ready to make a difference. The road ahead would be long, but with everybody's support, he felt unstoppable.

CHAPTER 10
FIRST SWEAT, THEN BLOOD, FINALLY SUCCESS

Once, Chetan accompanied Aryan to a major political function, an extravagant affair held in a lavish banquet hall that sparkled with ambition and influence. Aryan had sponsored numerous events like this, not just to solidify his political connections but also to ensure that Chetan, his mentor and friend, was celebrated in the spotlight he so richly deserved. As they entered the venue, the atmosphere buzzed with excitement, filled with well-dressed politicians, business leaders, and media personnel, all mingling under chandeliers that glimmered like stars.

But lurking in the shadows was a figure from Aryan's past—someone who recognized him from his darker days in the underworld. The moment their eyes met, a chill swept through the air, freezing the jubilant atmosphere around them. The man, with a sneer etched across his face, made his way through the crowd, drawing attention as he approached Aryan.

"Look who it is!" he shouted, his voice slicing through the chatter like a knife. "The reformed criminal turned politician! You really think you can just erase your past?"

Chetan's heart raced. He stepped closer to Aryan, sensing the impending storm, ready to shield him from the fallout. Aryan's expression hardened, a mix of anger and determination flickering in his eyes as he faced the man. "I'm not that person anymore. I've worked too hard to build a life that I'm proud of."

The crowd began to hush, their laughter fading as they realized a confrontation was brewing. The man's presence felt like a dark cloud hovering over the festivities, threatening to tarnish Aryan's hard-earned reputation. Whispers rippled through the attendees, eyes darting between Aryan and the unwelcome intruder.

"Maybe you've changed," the man continued, his tone dripping with contempt, "but everyone knows the truth. You're still the same thug underneath, flanked and supported by people like your friend over here. This is just a façade." He gestured toward Chetan, aiming to draw him into the fray.

In that moment, Aryan's protective instincts surged. He couldn't let Chetan be dragged into this mess. Chetan had stood by him through thick and thin, guiding him through the darkest times. Aryan's voice rose above the tension, fierce and unwavering. "I won't let you disrespect the people who matter to me. Back off."

The tension in the room escalated, palpable as silence enveloped them. Chetan felt Aryan's anger radiating, and he placed a steadying hand on Aryan's shoulder, his presence a reminder of their bond. "This isn't the time or place for this," Chetan said, his voice calm but firm. "Let's not give him the satisfaction."

The man scoffed, his laughter dripping with derision, but a flicker of hesitation crossed his face as Aryan's allies, sensing the charged atmosphere, began to encircle them like wolves ready to pounce. One influential figure stepped forward, his presence commanding yet measured. "Let's keep this civil," he intoned, his voice smooth like silk but laced with an undercurrent of steel. "We're here to celebrate, not to air old grievances."

The tension hung in the air, thick as smoke, refusing to dissipate. Aryan's heart thundered in his chest, adrenaline surging through his veins like wildfire as he locked eyes with the man, unyielding and fierce. This was not just a battle for his own dignity; it was a desperate fight to shield Chetan, the architect of his transformation. The stakes were monumental—this was about preserving his friends' respect, a sacred bond that could shatter with a single misstep.

"Everyone deserves a second chance," Chetan declared, stepping forward, a bastion of calm in a storm of hostility. His voice was steady, like the ground beneath their feet, yet it carried the weight of conviction that resonated in every corner of the room. "You don't define Aryan. His actions now speak louder than your hollow words."

A storm brewed in the man's eyes, irritation flaring like a dark cloud, but ultimately, he relented, muttering curses under his breath as he retreated into the crowd, leaving a trail of tension in his wake. Aryan felt the weight lift slightly, a fragile victory, but deep down he knew the encounter had carved scars—reminders of the battles fought and those yet to come.

As the atmosphere began to stabilize, Aryan turned to Chetan, his voice a low rumble filled with urgency. "I'm so sorry you had to witness that. I can't let anyone speak about you like that, especially not someone from my past." His eyes burned with a fierce protectiveness; a fire ignited by the confrontation.

Chetan placed a reassuring hand on Aryan's shoulder, grounding him amidst the storm of emotions. "You handled it well," he said, his voice calm and steady, like an anchor in turbulent waters. "Just remember, I'm in this with you. We all have our histories, but that doesn't dictate our futures." His words resonated with a depth of understanding, wrapping around Aryan like a shield against doubt.

In that moment, Aryan felt a wave of clarity wash over him. Despite the strides he had made, the shadows of his past were ever-present, lurking in the corners of his mind, threatening to engulf him. But with Chetan standing firm beside him, a pillar of support, he felt emboldened to confront whatever challenges lay ahead.

Later that evening, as they sat across from each other at a cozy table in the softly lit restaurant, Aryan savoured his meal, but his mind was on something deeper. He looked up from his plate, curiosity etched on his face. "Chetan, I've been meaning to ask you," he said, leaning slightly forward. "You had a thriving career, and now you've chosen this path of guiding and mentoring. What made you turn away from the corporate world? What's behind this newfound spirituality?"

Chetan paused, setting down his fork. The question was loaded, and he took a moment to reflect. "You know, Aryan," he began slowly, "for a long time, I was consumed by the idea of success as defined by society—climbing the corporate ladder, achieving accolades, accumulating wealth. I thought that was what would bring me happiness."

He glanced around the restaurant, observing the laughter and chatter, before returning his gaze to Aryan. "But there came a point when I realized that success in the material sense felt hollow. I was busy chasing goals but losing touch with what truly mattered. Connection, purpose, and impact."

Aryan nodded, intrigued. "Was there a specific moment that triggered this change?"

Chetan smiled softly. "Yes, actually. It was during a visit to a remote village in Africa. I was there to help with a development project, and what I saw changed everything. The people there lived simply, yet they radiated joy and community. They had little in terms of material possessions, but their sense of gratitude and togetherness was profound. It made me question everything I had been pursuing."

He leaned back, letting the weight of his words settle. "I realized that I wanted more than just personal success. I wanted to make a difference in the lives of others. So, I began to explore spirituality. Not as a retreat from the world, but as a way to engage with it more deeply. I wanted to help others find their paths, share my knowledge, and cultivate a sense of community."

Aryan took a sip of his drink, absorbing Chetan's revelations. "But isn't that risky? You had everything, financial security, status. Why give it up?"

Chetan chuckled lightly, shaking his head. "It's not about giving up; it's about evolving. I still apply my skills and experience, but now I focus on fostering growth and resilience in others. There's a thrill in guiding someone through their struggles, seeing them succeed. It's a different kind of success, one achieved by service and compassion."

"Sounds fulfilling," Aryan said thoughtfully. "But how do you reconcile the pressures of the world with your spiritual path?"

Chetan smiled warmly. "It's a balance. I believe we can be both grounded in our spiritual values and active in the world. I want to help people navigate their challenges while encouraging them to find deeper meaning in their lives. That's what drives me now."

Aryan looked at Chetan, admiration shining in his eyes. "You've always had a way of seeing beyond the surface. I respect your journey, my friend. It takes courage to redefine success."

Chetan's expression softened. "Thank you, Aryan. And remember, it's not just about me. We all have the power to create positive change. It's about lifting each other up and building a better future together."

As they continued their dinner, the conversation flowed seamlessly, bridging the gap between their pasts and the futures they both aspired to shape. Aryan, who wanted to shape the world politically, whereas Chetan wanted to do the same, spiritually.

The experience in that village became a turning point, a catalyst for a life that transcended the transactional. Chetan found joy in simplicity, community, and the beauty of human connection—elements that had always been present but often overlooked in his relentless pursuit of success. And so, he embarked on a new journey, one that promised not just personal fulfilment but a meaningful contribution to the world around him.

Over the next few months, Aryan's political journey skyrocketed. His charisma, dedication, and genuine connection with the people won him accolades far and wide. His reputation as a reformer became solidified, and he was soon appointed as a minister in his state. It was a position that not only elevated his status but also allowed him to implement the changes he had long envisioned.

As he settled into his new role, Aryan felt a great sense of purpose. He focused on pressing issues like education, healthcare, and infrastructure, striving to improve the lives of his constituents. His relentless work ethic and authentic leadership earned him the love and loyalty of the public, and soon his popularity became a phenomenon.

In the last elections, Aryan faced a situation unlike any other. He was elected unopposed. The opposing parties, recognizing the immense support he garnered from the community, opted not to field any candidates against him. They knew they stood no chance against a leader who had become synonymous with hope and progress. The streets were filled with celebration as Aryan's name echoed through the air; it was a clear message from the electorate: he was their choice, their mandate.

The announcement came on a sunny afternoon, and Aryan stood before a jubilant crowd that had gathered outside the assembly. His heart swelled with gratitude and determination. "This victory is not mine alone," he proclaimed, his voice resonating through the cheers. "It belongs to every single one of you! Together, we will build a future that we deserve. We will prove to the rest of the world that we aren't behind any of them!"

As he looked out at the sea of faces, Aryan felt the weight of responsibility settle on his shoulders. He remembered the challenges he had faced and the journey that had brought him here, from a troubled past to a leader of the people.

However, the pressure from the Chief Minister loomed like a dark cloud, growing increasingly oppressive. The head of Aryan's party was notorious for wielding his power like a weapon, extracting undue favours from cabinet ministers with ruthless efficiency. Contracts and tenders flowed in exchange for hefty bribes, an unspoken code of corruption that bound their ranks. In the ruthless world of politics, funding was the lifeblood for campaign advertisements and for supporting local party operatives.

Despite the seductive allure of power and its attendant perks, Aryan found himself at a harrowing moral crossroads. Charged with a vital ministry portfolio, he had painstakingly built a reputation for integrity and an unwavering commitment to the people. He would not compromise his principles for the sake of filling party coffers or enriching himself. His steadfast dedication to honesty and transparency often placed him at odds with the party's unscrupulous practices, and tensions escalated to a boiling point one fateful day.

In a heated confrontation with the Chief Minister, the air crackled with an electric tension. "You need to understand, Aryan, this is how things work!" the Chief Minister bellowed, his voice reverberating off the walls, filled with frustration and entitlement. "If you don't play the game, you'll be left behind."

Aryan stood his ground, fists clenched and heart pounding in his chest. "I won't sacrifice my integrity for the party's greed," he shot back, his voice steady but fierce. "We're supposed to serve the people, not exploit them for our gain. I refuse to be a part of this corruption!"

The argument escalated, a tempest of words and emotions, both men unwilling to relent. Aryan felt a surge of resolve wash over him like a tidal wave, drowning out the fear that threatened to creep in. It became painfully clear: he could no longer align himself with a system that so fundamentally contradicted his values. "I can't do this anymore. I'm resigning from the party," he declared, his voice unwavering, brimming with conviction.

The Chief Minister's eyes widened in disbelief, incredulous at the defiance before him. “You think you can just walk away? You’ll ruin your career!” he spat, venomous anger lacing his words.

“I’d rather ruin my career than lose my soul,” Aryan replied, his decision echoing like a battle cry.

With that, he stormed out of the meeting, heart racing with a chaotic mix of fear and exhilaration. The path ahead loomed daunting and fraught with challenges, yet within him burned an indomitable spirit. Aryan envisioned a new political party—one founded on the unwavering principles of honesty, transparency, and genuine service to the people. He knew the fight would be long and hard, but it was a fight worth waging, a rebellion against a system that had grown rotten at its core.

In the days that followed, Aryan became a whirlwind of energy and determination, rallying support from like-minded individuals who shared his fervent vision. He reached out to his constituents with an impassioned voice, fervently speaking about the urgent need for a political movement that genuinely represented the people’s interests—untainted by the corruption that had long plagued their system.

Aryan's vision for a new political party crystallized with astonishing speed. He meticulously curated a team of individuals who embodied his core values—honesty, integrity, and an unwavering commitment to uplift society. Each candidate was rigorously vetted, not just for their political acumen, but for their character and dedication to public service. This was not merely about politics; it was a crusade to reclaim their collective dignity.

While seasoned politicians and MLAs approached him with enticing offers, eager to latch onto his rising star, Aryan stood resolute in his mission. He turned down those whose pasts were stained with corruption or self-serving motives, resolutely focusing on a core group that reflected the ideals he sought to champion. This was a new dawn, and he was determined to ensure it wasn't clouded by the shadows of old transgressions.

As word of his movement spread, the momentum began to build—a groundswell of support from everyday citizens tired of the status quo. Town halls and community meetings buzzed with excitement, filled with voices that once felt silenced. Together, they envisioned a political landscape where integrity reigned, and the people's voices echoed loud and clear.

As the party began to gain traction, Aryan and his team worked tirelessly to connect with communities across the state. They listened to the concerns of the people—issues of unemployment, education, healthcare, and infrastructure. Each interaction fuelled Aryan's resolve to make real changes. He organized town hall meetings, held rallies, and engaged with grassroots movements, reaching out to the citizens.

The political climate was tense, a simmering cauldron of entrenched opposition. Established parties were rooted in their ways, using every dirty tactic in the book to maintain control. Yet, Aryan’s authenticity pierced through the noise, striking a chord with the public and igniting a groundswell of support. His message was unmistakable: this was a party for the people, a collective movement to forge a path toward a brighter future.

As the major election approached, the atmosphere crackled with electric anticipation. Aryan’s campaign radiated passion and principle, a stark contrast to the mudslinging and deceitful tactics of his opponents. The people recognized that Aryan was not just another candidate; he was a leader who genuinely cared about their struggles, someone who would fight for them in the halls of power.

On the day of the election, the air was thick with excitement and anxiety. Polling stations buzzed with eager voters, while Aryan's supporters flooded the streets, chanting for change and a new dawn. When the votes were finally tallied, the moment of truth arrived. Aryan's party emerged victorious, a triumphant testament to the power of integrity and unity. Cheers erupted, and tears of joy flowed as hope turned into reality, marking the beginning of a transformative journey for the state and its people.

When the results were announced, Aryan's heart swelled with an overwhelming tide of emotion. He hadn't just won an election; he had ignited a movement that reverberated through the hearts of thousands. As he stood before the jubilant crowd, their cheers echoing like a symphony of hope, he fully grasped the magnitude of what lay ahead. The mantle of leadership felt heavy, but it was a burden he was more than prepared to bear.

In that electrifying moment, Aryan transformed from a mere politician into the very embodiment of hope for those who had placed their trust in him. With his election as Chief Minister, he made a solemn vow to prioritize development, transparency, and the upliftment of the marginalized. The real work was just beginning, and Aryan was resolute, ready to lead with the same fierce determination and unwavering integrity that had propelled him this far.

His journey stood as a powerful testament to the resilience of the human spirit and the impact of perseverance. Aryan was committed to ensuring that every voice in his state was heard and valued, determined to dismantle the barriers that had long silenced the most vulnerable. With fire in his heart and clarity in his vision, he stepped into his role, ready to forge a future where hope wasn't just a dream, but a living reality for all.

Chetan had fully embraced his spiritual journey, discovering profound peace in a life that transcended the transactional nature of the world around him. His days were now rich with mindfulness, meditation, and a deep commitment to guiding those in need. Meanwhile, Aryan's sons had matured into capable young men, poised to shoulder the responsibilities of their father's expansive business empire.

On the day of Aryan's retirement, the atmosphere in the head office was charged with a bittersweet blend of emotion and celebration. Colleagues, friends, and family gathered, eager to witness this pivotal moment in Aryan's life. As he stood before the crowd, a swell of pride surged within him. This was not merely a farewell; it was a ceremonial passing of the torch to the next generation, a legacy being handed down.

Chetan was present, seated in the office cabin that had always held a special significance for them both. The room was adorned with a picture of Lord Ganesha, symbolizing wisdom and new beginnings, alongside Chetan's cemented footprints displayed in a glass enclosure—a poignant testament to their enduring friendship.

As Aryan entered the cabin, the two friends exchanged a warm embrace, their bond unbroken by the passage of time or distance. "I couldn't have done any of this without you, Chetan," Aryan said, his voice thick with emotion, a lump forming in his throat. "You've been my guiding light through it all."

Chetan smiled, a serene expression illuminating his face. "And you've created a legacy that will inspire others for years to come. I'm proud of you, Aryan." His words, simple yet profound, resonated deeply within Aryan's heart.

They took a moment to reflect, the weight of their shared past mingling with the promise of the future. Aryan's gaze fell on the footprints on the wall, symbols of where he had come from and how far he had travelled. "I've always wanted to make you proud, and I hope I've succeeded," he said, sincerity shining in his eyes.

"You've not only succeeded, but you've also changed lives," Chetan replied, his tone firm yet gentle. "You've shown that one can rise above their circumstances and create something meaningful. Remember, this is just another chapter. Your journey continues." His words hung in the air like a blessing, a reminder of the path that lay ahead.

As the celebration began to unfold outside, Aryan and Chetan shared stories, laughter, and dreams for the future. The warmth of their friendship enveloped them, a comforting reminder that their paths had always been intertwined. Aryan knew that no matter where life took them next, the values and lessons he had learned from Chetan would guide him through all his endeavours. Together, they had navigated the complexities of life, and now, as new chapters awaited, their bond would remain an unshakeable foundation, inspiring them both to forge ahead into the unknown.

As the party began to unfold outside, Aryan and Chetan shared stories, laughter, and dreams for the future. The warmth of friendship enveloped them, a reminder that their paths had always been intertwined. Aryan knew that no matter where life took them next, the values and lessons he had learned from Chetan would guide him in all his endeavours.

That day marked not just the end of Aryan's corporate journey, but also the beginning of a new chapter filled with potential, purpose, and a commitment to uplift others, just as Chetan had always done. And Chetan, well he continues to touch lives through his guidance and mentoring. And where he cannot reach himself, his books do.

Printed in Dunstable, United Kingdom